# Remembering Love

## By
## Nadine Christian

Eternal Press
A division of Damnation Books, LLC.
P.O. Box 3931
Santa Rosa, CA 95402-9998
www.eternalpress.biz

Remembering Love
by Nadine Christian

Digital ISBN: 978-1-61572-854-1
Print ISBN: 978-1-61572-855-8

Cover art by: Dawné Dominique
Edited by: Carrie Ro

Printed in the United States of America
Worldwide Electronic & Digital Rights
1st North American, Australian and UK Print Rights

This book is a work of fiction. Characters, names,
places and incidents either are the product of the
author's imagination or are used fictitiously, and any
resemblance to any actual persons, living or dead,
events, or locales is entirely coincidental.

*For all those who believed in me: My husband and children, my Mollusk—you know who you are—who hugged me when I was down, pushed me to go that extra mile when I was reluctant, and was my own private cheerleader when everything went well.*

*Thank you to Pitcairn Island, my muse, my home, my island.*

*Most of all, thank you to Eternal Press for taking the chance on a first-time Author, who cannot believe she's actually typing that word to describe herself.*

# Prologue

A blond haired cherub of a girl sat, ears perked, listening for her hunter. Hands stifling small sounds that escaped unbidden, she covered her mouth. She moved duck-like backward, further into her hidey-hole. The perfect place to play and hide, the banyan tree had formed an alcove so deep and so well disguised by overhanging branches and leaves that she'd only found it by accident. Light shone feebly through the foliage, the further back she went the darker it got. Now if only she could stay quiet long enough and not let the fear of the darkness push her back out, he'd never find her.

Leaves crackled as her hunter tracked her, passed her hiding place and moved on.

Heart beating fast in her chest, fear easing slightly as he moved away, she moved forward an inch or two, into shafts of sunlight that filtered weakly through the roots that formed wooden, jail cell bars. Peering out, left and right, she saw nothing bar more banyan giants, dried leaves and dirt pathways. A smile slowly crossed her chubby face. She was safe.

"Raah!"

An avalanche of leaves, sticks, and stones cascaded between the banyan roots as a brown haired grenade, cannon-balled into a nest of leaves with a bloodcurdling yell, right in front of her hidey-hole.

"I found you! I found you! Your turn to hide, Holly!"

If she could have, in the small space, Holly would have stamped her foot in frustration. She frowned at the freckled faced boy who lay laughing in the leaves and did the next best thing. She sat with a plop in the dirt and crossed her arms, lips pouting disagreeably.

"You cheated, Jack."

He grinned a crooked grin, eyes twinkling with mischief at his best friend and shook his head, peering in at his foe through the banyan roots. "You shouldn't have moved dummy. I saw your yellow hair."

She put her nose in the air with a sniff and turned her face from him, lips turning down in the corners of her mouth with consternation. "Whatever. I know you cheated somehow."

*He was such a know-it-all. Just because he was older than she was didn't mean he knew everything. He was so frustrating—and quiet. What was he doing?* She snuck a look and burst into uncontrollable giggles. He'd pressed his face into a gap between the roots and was crossing his eyes and poking out his tongue, stretching the skin of his face into a grotesque mask, index finger pushing up the tip of his nose.

He jigged with repressed laughter as he snorted at her. "Hey, piggy, piggy—come out of your cage," he chanted.

"Better stop that. My mummy says, if the wind changes you'll stay like that," she said with a giggle.

Across the valley angry voices echoed into the gully of banyans—a woman's voice, shrill and accusing, a male's, thick with rage.

Jack looked toward the sound, mouth open, eyes wide, frozen in place. Holly watched his stricken face carefully, glad they were hidden from sight, glad she could not make out the muffled words. That meant he couldn't either.

She tipped her head to one side. He looked like he'd never heard adults yell like that. These voices were familiar to her. Too familiar—they were her parents. They yelled like that all the time, but, they were getting louder, and that meant other things would happen.

If only Mummy would just come outside, run away, come hide in the banyan with her. He couldn't yell at her if she wasn't there—couldn't find her.

Jack glanced sidelong at her. Then did a double-take. "Are you scared? It's okay, they're not yelling at you."

She closed her eyes against *that* look. He had that same sad face that Mummy had after Daddy growled at her. Holly almost wished he was pulling a silly face again, she *hated* that sad face. It meant that someone was hurting, usually tears followed. Her Mummy was always crying.

Holly folded into herself, curling up her legs and clamping her arms around her knees. She began to rock as the voices grew louder and more strident. This one was *really* bad. They were normally a little more discreet about their arguments, it wasn't good to let the neighbors overhear.

"Is that your mum and dad?" he whispered. It wasn't a question really. Holly knew he already knew the answer.

Her blue eyes brimmed with unshed tears as she nodded mutely. They were always fighting. They didn't even see her anymore.

They used to go outside and yell at each other, as if they thought she couldn't hear them through the thin clapboard walls. Now they just yelled whether she was there or not.

She hadn't told Jack. She'd wanted to, but she had not known how to say the words. He was the only one she dared even *thinking* about talking to. She knew that complaining to grown-ups wouldn't help; they'd never listen to someone as little as her.

\* \* \* \*

Jack squeezed into the alcove and sat next to the quiet girl as the tears began to drip unchecked down her cheeks. Putting his arm around her he pulled her into his skinny frame as she began to tremble. He swayed in time with her unconscious movement.

"We'll just stay here for a while huh?" he asked. Holly's mute fear infecting him by osmosis.

The woman's voice got louder and more high-pitched as she screeched accusations and recriminations. He couldn't hear exactly what they were saying, but she was royally pissed about something. Jack winced as the man let a string of swear words fly. He certainly got that loud and clear. A door slammed, the voices became louder, easier to understand. He wished they'd stayed inside as his mouth dropped open. Vicious words made the girl clap her hands over her ears, and sent chills down the boy's spine.

A sudden silence descended over the thicket of trees and the boy relaxed a little. *Maybe they'd gone back inside.*

He'd heard his own parents discussing the girl's mum and dad once. He'd been on his way to the bathroom one night and passed their bedroom door while they were lying in bed talking. He'd overheard Holly's name and had stopped in his tracks to listen, full bladder complaining.

Pressing up against the wall in the darkened hallway, he'd listened, not understanding most of what they said, but knowing they felt pity for his friend's situation. He wondered, with annoyance for his friend, if they were worried why they didn't do something about it?

He was startled out of his reverie as the quiet was broken with a sharp cry from the woman. The female's voice sounded like the woman was right outside their hiding place and Jack scooted backward into the dark, dragging the girl in deeper with him. Holly began to tremble violently under his tight embrace. He pulled her in even tighter in his embrace, unsure if he was trying to comfort himself, or her. The cries from the woman became frantic, panic filled. One word repeated over and over. "No! I'm not! Sammy! No!"

A gunshot, birds flew out of the branches above and around them in panic, the air filled with the noise of wings beating, and the sudden howling cry of the girl in his arms, rigid with terror. A male's agonized wail competed with Holly's screams, standing the hairs on Jack's arm up in horror.

Another gunshot rang out. A final sharp retort, and then silence.

# Chapter One

Holly let the heavy suitcases fall out of her hands and land with a double thud on the paved driveway. She turned her heart shaped face to the sun, closing her eyes tight against the glare, enjoying the heat on her face. She rolled her head and then her shoulders, rotating her arms; they felt as if they were nearly pulled from their sockets.

Gazing down at her hands she sighed. Being slender with a build not used to carrying heavy loads, the weight of the cases handles had left bright red welts in her palms. She rubbed her hands together like a miser gloating over a pile of money, trying to get feeling back into unfeeling fingers.

Shaking the last of the numbness out of her hands she stood placing them on her slim hips and looked up at the old clapboard house. In the bright morning sunlight its gabled roof and wooden exterior appeared haggard and tired. The place screamed desperately for a coat of paint and some good old fashioned elbow grease—or alternatively a wrecking ball.

She smiled wearily; the house looked like she felt—exhausted.

It had been a five day journey born from hell. A turbulent flight from New Zealand to Tahiti and three nights spent awaiting a flight from Tahiti to the Gambier Islands. Two days more were spent crossing the Pacific Ocean in seas so rough even the soaked crew were turning green. Now, here she stood in front of her childhood home on Pitcairn Island that she didn't even remember. Heck, she'd not even known Pitcairn itself existed until three months ago.

Brought up in New Zealand in the loving bosom of a Kiwi foster family, all she'd known was love, support and extended family. Foster kids roamed a house which was ruled by a firm but fair elderly couple who came from trouble backgrounds themselves and knew the system well.

Over the years Holly watched Bill and Tina take in many problem children that no one else could handle and raise them with love, expecting nothing but trust, honesty ,and respect in return. Some caused years of disappointment, but were loved anyway. Some caused years of joy, and gave reason for taking in yet another lost child.

Holly came to them a sullen, traumatized child with no memory of her past life. Thinking this a blessing considering all she went through, Bill and Tina thought it best to tell her as little as possible. So Holly grew up with the knowledge her parents had both died, but unaware of the circumstances of their passing. Bill and Tina nurtured and encouraged the little girl in their care and the natural resilience of a young child shone through the broken five-year-old they had first welcomed into their foster home. Holly blossomed as a result of their patience and understanding.

With their encouragement and prompting she excelled in school, graduating from College with honors in English and Literature. Accepted into the prestigious University of Otago, she received her diploma with her foster parents standing proud beside her. A few years later they stood again full of pride beside her as she accepted a prize for the Best Young Writer of the year for her first novel.

They marveled at how well their daughter had done, holding her up as an example to each new foster child that walked through their door, not accepting any praise for all the support or for the foundations they themselves had laid over the years. She'd proved yet again that even the most broken child could do anything they put their mind to if given the love they deserved.

For Holly, it was an idyllic childhood, full of love and encouragement. It was only when her beloved foster parents passed away that she found out the truth of her past.

Together with her many foster brothers and sisters they'd tearfully begun sifting through their universally loved parent's home. Packing up much used and well-worn furniture for donation to a charitable trust, they kept out treasures from their childhood toys and books to save for themselves. Laughter, mixed with tears, filled the house as they filtered through children's drawings, artwork, and boxes of photos showing years of birthdays, holidays at the beach, and finally graduations and weddings.

At the end of one long, dusty day sorting the last of the boxes from the attic, Holly found a box marked with her name amongst a pile of miscellaneous cartons. Sitting weary and deeply curious, she pulled the box toward her. The dust kicked as she dragged the box across the attic floor, flittering through the shafts of sunlight that shone through the skylights. Tucking a loose tendril of long, blond hair behind her ear she clicked open a box cutter and sliced the tape sealing the box closed.

Thrilled at finding a treasure specifically marked for her, she opened a Pandora's Box of her past. A birth announcement in the Pitcairn Island newspaper called the *Miscellany*. A yellowed and creased birth certificate for a baby girl born on Pitcairn—Holly Marie Christian. Photos of a happy family, she didn't recognize, but knew with uncanny instinct that she was part of. The mother, father, and baby— the baby growing, here a one year old, a two year old, three. The girl in the photo always happy, blond hair in ringlets, pony-tails, pig-tails, freckles across a turned up nose, bowed lips pursed into smiles, grins, or laughing toothily.

With a start she brought one photo closer to her face to study. Moving quickly to a brighter patch of sunlight she studied a slightly faded and creased photo of a blond haired woman coddling a small child. The woman was grinning with a radiant smile at the person behind the camera, turning the baby just so, arranging the infant so the camera could see. The woman in the picture could have been Holly herself sitting for this posed shot. The hair was styled differently, but same heart shaped face, and *there*, her own green eyes stared out at her.

Tears prickled beneath her lashes. This was her mother. She held the photo to her chest and closed her eyes against a rush of loss and painful regret. The dream of a reunion with her parents had never been one she'd been able to hang on to as a foster kid knowing they'd passed away, but she'd always wondered where she'd come from, what they'd been like. She felt a momentary pang of anger at her foster parents for not showing her this earlier. She'd never known this woman, she never would, but at least she could have known what she looked like. She turned back to the box and pulled out more papers, now eager to find out more about her.

Pulling out some yellowed and tatty paper she found the probable explanation as to why she was never given any more information than was absolutely necessary. With a start she realized this article must have been saved for a reason. She laid the paper in her lap and smoothed her hair absentmindedly. She almost didn't want to know what was written here. She shook her head. "Don't be silly," she muttered under her breath. This was what all foster kids wanted to know wasn't it? The past? The reason why they were put into foster care?

With a grimace she picked up the paper with shaking hands betraying her trepidation. Shock set in as she read of a murder/suicide on Pitcairn Island, a child left an orphan. Grainy newspaper photos of a clapboard house, a crying, blonde haired child being sheltered from the camera by an adult male, a snarl permanently captured by the photographer's viewfinder.

Pitcairn Island. A.P. Murder / Suicide reported this week on Pitcairn Island.

Pitcairn, one of the most isolated British Overseas Territories today finally released information regarding the grisly murder of Celeste Christian by her husband Samuel John Christian, who consequently committed suicide. This reporter asks; was it remorse or guilt?

Citing investigation difficulties due to extreme isolation and lack of criminal forensic facilities the obvious case of murder / suicide has now been closed.

An anonymous source revealed that the couple were constantly fighting, often coming to blows. Police on island when asked confirmed, "Domestic incidents in the past were reported and thoroughly investigated."

Police report that Mrs. Christian was discovered with a fatal shotgun wound to the chest last Thursday just outside the couples Pitcairn Island home—tragically, by her five year old daughter. Mister Christian, with a self-inflicted and also fatal gunshot wound was found slumped nearby.

The child, who has been granted name suppression by the courts, has been removed from the island and placed in foster care.

One of Holly's foster sisters found her sitting in the darkened attic, dry eyed and stunned a few hours later. The proof sat crumpled in her hands, who she was, what had happened—but nothing seemed real. She had no memories of this girl, Holly Marie Christian, though that's who she was. She had no memories of Pitcairn Island, yet that was where she was born, where she lived for five years. She'd sat for hours trying to remember anything, *something* of her childhood. All that remained was a black void that refused to shed any light before she was thrust into the loving arms of her foster family.

Rosanna pulled over a box and sat beside her aware that something was very wrong. "What's up Holl?"

Holly and Rosanna had been put in foster care with Bill and Tina around the same time and were around the same age. Though their years had been the same, they were two very different people. Olive skinned, dark haired, wiry like a bull terrier, and full of the same attitude. Rosanna was the smart-aleck kid that had the answer for anything, the balls to stand up to kids twice her age, and there would be hell to pay if you crossed her. Befriending the silent Holly, she'd been the one who'd bullied her with kindness, bringing her out of her shell. Where one would be you'd find the other.

Holly dumped the documents in Rosanna's lap. "Read it Rosy."

Raising an eyebrow she shuffled quickly through the papers, hovering longer over the newspaper article, digesting the information with sick horror for her sister.

"Geez, would have been nice to find this out earlier."

"No kidding."

Holly looked at her sister as tears began to well in her eyes. "Who am I?"

\* \* \* \*

Holly stumbled through the next month, just barely existing. Writing, normally a natural part of her day, suffered. Where she'd normally write for a few hours, she sat in front of her laptop just staring at a blank screen, cursor blinking irritatingly at her. Words failed to sooth as they usually did, now jeering at her with the lack of them. Finally she gave up. Packed the laptop in its case and zipped it closed with frustration.

Discouraged, Holly took a menial job in a fast food restaurant just to get out of the house and away from the computer and its incessant silent mocking of her inability to put two words together.

Work, home, eat, sleep, wake up, and begin again. It was as if someone had taken a blackboard filled with the story of her life and wiped it clean. She swung from irrational anger with her foster parents for withholding her past to grateful relief that they did.

One Saturday morning she awoke from a sleep filled with dreams she couldn't remember to an urgent knocking on the door. Stumbling through her apartment, rubbing sleep filled eyes, she opened the door to an excited Rosy. She carried an armful of books, a mysterious bag, and she looked fit to burst with pent up excitement.

"Let me in sleepyhead." She looked at her watch pointedly as she brushed past Holly. "It's after nine, what are you still doing in bed?"

"It's the weekend. I'm allowed." Holly grinned and flicked the kettle on, grabbing two cups off the shelf. "When have you ever been up before nine anyway?"

"Since I started researching Pitcairn." She pointed at the coffee jar. "Make mine strong. Yours too, you'll need it." She spread the papers and books she'd collected over the dining room table.

Rosy's research at the library reading archived newspapers and speaking to the Commissioner at the Pitcairn Island Administration Office based in Auckland had revealed nothing new. Too much time had passed and no one in official circles knew anything bar what the newspapers had already reported.

"You should go." Rosy sipped her coffee and watched Holly carefully over the rim of her mug as she flipped through a book on Pitcairn.

"Go where? Pitcairn?" Holly was taken aback. "What is there that would make me want to go back Rosy, gravestones?"

Rosy frowned and thumped her cup down on the table slopping her coffee over the side. Glaring at her sister as she sopped up the mess with a dish towel, she spoke her mind. "Holl, you have something to go back to—most of us don't. The Commissioner said there's a house held in trust for you, you've got a history there. Go find it."

Rosy paused, gazing down at her hands which coddled the half full cup, trying to hide her own unhappiness. "You've got more from your parents than I ever did, and mine are still alive."

Holly slumped down in her chair, reprimanding herself with disgust. Here she was feeling sorry for herself and forgetting how lucky she was. Rosy was right—at least she had two sets of parents that had loved her, even if the first set were genuinely messed up.

"Sorry Rosy."

"Just think about it. Seriously. There's a supply ship due to travel to Pitcairn in a couple of months—be on it. You owe it to yourself to at least find out where you're from."

Holly stared at her sister blankly for a moment. If she was honest with herself, this was something she'd already been thinking about, tossing around in her subconscious like a plaything. Rosy saying the words out loud like this just made it all the more sensible and sane to her. "Okay. When you're right, you're right. I'll go."

Rosy pumped her fists in celebration, smiling a self-satisfied smile. Holly grinned. Her sister always had to have her own way—even if it was someone else's life she was organizing.

\* \* \* \*

Preparations to go 'home' were remarkably difficult and long winded. Forms and paperwork had to be filled out, although it was made easier with the presentation of the Pitcairn birth certificate to prove her heritage. The Claymore was the only way on or off the island, a quarterly supply ship that carried cargo to restock the islands stores and supplies.

Now as she stood in front of a house that seemed so alien and yet astonishingly familiar, she seemed frozen to the spot. The day was hot, sultry with tropical breezes that barely lifted her long hair from her damp neck, but she shivered none the less. She shook herself, giggled at her silly unproven fears and picked up her suitcases with a groan.

The house was set in a valley just out of Adamstown, the only town on Pitcairn. Most homes were situated here, although some sat nestled higher in the hills out of town. Her parent's house was on its own surrounded by mango and banana trees on one side and a stand of huge banyan trees on the other. Neighbors and the actual town square was a ten minute walk away. The only noise here now was the sounds of birds, distant rumble of ATV bikes and the scuff of her feet on the pavers as she walked up the drive.

She'd been dropped off here by one of the locals curious to know everything about her in the twenty minute drive from the landing, but didn't stop talking long enough for her to answer any of the multitudes of questions. She was glad because she couldn't have answered any even if she'd wanted to. She didn't have the answers herself.

In fact there had been an army of curious locals at the landing when the longboat had pulled alongside the wharf. With an island population of around sixty it seemed as if they'd all turned up to check her out. Her notorious past and sudden arrival on the island had made her something of a twisted celebrity. Something different to talk about.

The passenger ship Claymore had arrived early morning to calm seas in Bounty Bay after a very choppy crossing from the Mangarevan port in the Gambier Islands. Heavy with six foot containers full of supplies for the island, the ship had rolled and lurched through the Pacific. The calm seas this morning boded well for unloading today. Holly realized with relief that unloading of cargo was probably the only reason she was alone now. The community was all busy.

Holly hesitated on the threshold of the house. Waited for some sign or flash of recognition of the porch, front door, handle, *anything. Nothing.*

Laughing at herself for being so silly, she opened the door and walked into her childhood home. Opening up to a large lounge area, the house was bare of family touches. The inside had the same air as the outside. Sad, unlived in, and tired.

Leaving her bags by the open door she explored her new abode. A smallish kitchen, where someone had left freshly baked bread wrapped in a cloth on the bench and fresh fruit in a bowl. Three bedrooms, one bare of furniture, one with a bed nicely made up and set of drawers—obviously the very same welcome fairy that left the items in the kitchen had been busy in here too. She smiled at the thoughtfulness.

The last bedroom was full of clutter, boxes, plastic bags bulging with unidentified objects, picture frames, and more boxes. It looked as though someone had packed up the personal items and things that made the house a home and shoved it in here. She closed the door firmly on the chaos and turned her back on it. There was time enough to sort through that mess later.

Switching on the kettle and dumping her bags in her room she opened all the windows and doors to let air circulate. Standing at the kitchen sink and looking blindly out the window she waited for the water to boil. Now she was here she mused, what next? Would there be some clue to be found in the junk room? Would someone here still know her story? Or her parents story?

Opening the fridge door she found a packet of long life milk for her coffee, but also noted the fresh eggs and a pot of butter. Her welcome fairy had been busy here too. She wondered who she had to thank.

When she'd arranged to stay in her parents' house she had been told that it had been well looked after by the islanders. In fact, it had been lived in by a young local family for years. Without rental accommodation on island any vacant house was utilized. If not, the house would have disappeared beneath the verdant growth of Pitcairn vine and weeds long ago.

Holly spent the afternoon unpacking and cleaning, throwing covers over the threadbare couches and trying to put her own stamp on the house as much as she could with the little she'd brought. One item though cried out to her in particular. She pulled out her laptop from its carry case and laid it gently on the kitchen table. Plugging it in to recharge she sat down to flick Rosy an email to let her know she was safe, and then logged off. There was no way she was going to try and write today. She was wiping down the kitchen windows when a sharp rap on the door and a cheery hello alerted her to her first visitor.

Tucking an errant wisp of hair behind her ear she poked her head around the kitchen door. A tall, dark haired, well-built man leaned casually against the doorjamb. A large grin on his face, his brown eyes sparkling, he seemed happy to see her.

"Remember me?"

Holly walked up to greet him, shaking her head with a confused smile. Reaching out to shake his hand she shrugged apologetically. "No, sorry—should I?"

He reached out and shook her hand with a strong grip and frowned with disappointment. "I was hoping." He scratched at the five o'clock shadow on his chin. "We used to follow each other around like a bad smell when we were kids." He looked into her eyes curiously. "You sure you don't remember me? Jack?"

Holly stared up at the tall man hoping not to disappoint him further, searching his face, his brown eyes and short brown hair, full mouth, strong stubbly chin. Attractive maybe, but nothing rang a bell. If they were friends when they were kids he would have changed a hell of a lot in twenty odd years though.

"It was a long time ago, Jack." She shrugged and stepped back to welcome him in. "It's what I'm here for I guess. To remember."

Jack followed her into the kitchen. "I've just popped over to show you how to get hot water, and basically to invite you over for dinner. Until you shop the cupboards will be a bit bare."

"Thanks. Someone's already been busy." She motioned to the fresh bread and fruit. She'd already tucked into some of the bananas. They were about half the size of the ones in the shop in New Zealand, and twice as sweet. She could live on those alone for a while she thought with a grin to herself.

"A few people came down to get things ready for you. You're a bit of an enigma here at the moment." He grinned and crossed his arms over his chest. "I'm surprised I didn't find the house full of people."

Holly grinned right back. His smile was infectious. "Me too," she said with a laugh. "People were staring like I had three heads when I got off the boat this morning."

"They'll get over it. There's always something to talk about on Pitcairn." He clapped his hands and rubbed them together. "Right. I'll show you how to light the copper."

The hot water system was not much more than a drum, suspended over a fire, surround by a concrete enclosure. The old fashioned system was cheap to run burning only firewood, and didn't rely on the power grid which she'd been advised only ran fourteen hours a day. That alone was going to take some getting used to she thought with a wry grin.

As Jack made to leave giving her directions to his house and recommending carrying a torch for the walk back, he stopped and peered hard at her.

"I'll help you remember if you want Holly." He smiled sadly, brow furrowed. "Although, some things are best forgotten."

His smile turned cheeky and he dropped a wink at her. "But, I'm definitely someone you should remember."

\* \* \* \*

Jack walked the short distance home with a hop in his step. He'd never forgotten his childhood friend; they'd been thicker than thieves and twice as mischievous. She'd changed from the little girl he'd once known of course, but he was looking forward to getting to know her again. He began to whistle cheerfully as he walked and remembered her smile as he left. Yes, he would enjoy getting to know her again—very much.

# Chapter Two

Jack opened the door with a flourish, and motioned her in. Holly found the house easily with Jack's directions. A short walk down the unpaved, dirt roads, past the banyan trees, and up a small turn off, led to a tidy clapboard house, not unlike her own. Lights shone warmly in the windows in the twilight of the evening.

Making her comfortable at a breakfast bar in the kitchen, he stirred a pot bubbling merrily on the stove, dishcloth thrown jauntily across one shoulder. He was freshly shaven and just out of the shower. As he bent down next to her to grab something out of the cupboard, she realized with a jolt he smelled great too. Her cheeks flushed and she quickly looked away from him before he noticed. Alarm bells rang stridently in her head as she felt a buzz of excitement deep in her belly, a loosening in her loins. *What the hell's going on here*, she wondered giddily.

Whatever he had cooked smelled heavenly and made Holly's stomach rumble alarmingly. She giggled to herself. *No matter what muddle my mind is in, trust my belly to change the subject*, she thought.

"I hope you're hungry." He said with a smile. "Just waiting for Dad to get ready and we'll eat."

While he poured her a glass of wine and set the table Jack chattered about his day, and she sat listening and watching him potter around the kitchen.

Jack explained that he had moved back home a few months before and was looking after his father who was in the early stages of Alzheimer's. He had his own house further up the hill, but had closed it up once he'd realized his father's progressing forgetfulness wasn't as simple as lost keys and forgotten appointments.

"For a long time I thought it was just Dad not coping with Mum being gone. She passed away just over a year ago. I felt guilty as hell when I realized it was more than that." He paused and sipped at his own wine. "Poor Dad, he was always a strong minded, vital man. Kills me to see his intelligence and awareness slowly disappearing."

"It must be hard all on your own," Holly said.

"Nah," he replied, swatting the compliment away like a fly. "I have help. One of the local women comes in every day to watch him so I can go to work, or have a break."

Holly watched as he moved confidently around the kitchen as he spoke and she sipped at her wine. Even with the confusion whirling around in her brain about the reaction her traitorous body had to him, she still found herself unexplainably at ease with this man, essentially still a stranger to her. Here she was on a strange island, in a strange house, and she felt weirdly at home, it was if she was sitting in Rosy's kitchen—familiar. She hopped down off her stool to check out a wall of framed family photos. Jack moved to stand beside her.

Family portraits and graduation photos graced the wall. A photo that looked two or three years old was pride of place. In the center, a younger Jack, four middle aged men and women and two elderly people—obviously his parents—stood in a formal photo, it looked like in the town square. Pointing to the four older people Holly asked, "Your brothers and sisters?"

"Yeah, I was a surprise," he said with a laugh. "Mum and Dad thought that their child rearing days were over and all of a sudden there I was."

"That photo was taken a couple of years before Mum died. Everyone came home for Christmas that year; first time in a long time that we were all together." A wistful softness entered his voice. "She was over the moon that they'd all made the effort to come back; they've all got good jobs and family. You know how hard it is to get here."

Holly nodded. She certainly did. The trip took months to organize.

"I'm glad Mum's not here to watch Dad going downhill." He touched the frame absentmindedly with his finger, straightening the already neatly aligned photo sadly.

"I'm sorry about your Mum, Jack. You seem to be stuck between a rock and a hard place—losing your mother and then your dad falling ill." She put her hand on his arm in a show of sympathy.

Jack looked down at her, eyes soft with sadness. "You'd know loss and hardship better than I would."

"My foster parents died not so long ago. They were everything to me—and a lot of other foster kids."

"Your real parents too."

Holly shrugged. "I guess..."She paused trying to think of the right way to put her thoughts into words, twisting the stem of her wineglass in her hands. "I knew my foster parents. I can't remember my real parents...I only feel the void of my foster parents at the moment." She looked at Jack questioningly.

"Does that seem harsh?

He shook his head with a sigh. "Not really."

She laughed sadly suddenly realizing the morbid turn the conversation had taken. "Let's change the subject—please."

Jack grinned. "Okay. Well, how about I check on Dad, and we'll have some dinner?"

As Jack went to check on his father Holly continued to stare blankly at the wall of family photos. She wondered what her own would have looked like. Would she have had brothers and sisters? What would it have been like to grow up on the island?

She was all of a sudden angry with herself. She'd had a good life with Bill and Tina, she'd wanted for nothing. She'd had so many brothers and sisters that sometimes she'd wished to be an only child. There was no point asking useless questions that no one could answer. There was only finding answers to what had happened.

The shuffling of slippers and the murmur of Jack's voice in reply to a wavering question signaled the arrival of Jack's father. Jack led the elderly man into the kitchen, grey haired and shoulders stooped with time. He shuffled wearily beside his son, eyes glued to the floor.

"Dad, someone's joining us for dinner tonight." Jack pointed toward Holly, gently nudging his father to guide his father's gaze. Jack smiled as Holly stepped forward to meet them.

"This is my Dad, James."

Watery, brown eyes focused slowly on Holly, a smile widening as his eyes lit up with recognition.

"Celeste!"

Jack shot a look at Holly's shocked face and screwed up his face with an apology as he turned to his father. "No Dad, this is Holly. Celeste's daughter."

James glared at his son. "Don't be silly, Holly's just a child."

"Dad." Jack put his hands on both his father's shoulders and moved to stand in front of him, looking him dead in the eye. "This is Holly. She's grown up now. Celeste is gone—remember?"

James stared at his son in confusion. Flicking a glance at Holly as she stood unsure of how to react, he seemed to fold in on himself. He dropped his head. "Damn it all to hell," he mumbled.

Holly moved to grasp James hand as Jack dropped his hands from his father's shoulders with a sigh of frustration. He frowned apologetically. "I'm sorry Holly. Sometimes the past is clearer than the present and some days are better than others."

"It's okay—really. Why don't you serve dinner and I'll seat him." She smiled reassuringly at Jack even though her heart was beating fast in her chest at James's mistaking her for her mother. She hoped Jack wouldn't realize how terrified she actually was. It was like James had torn the scab off a festering wound that she'd not known she'd had. She felt a desperate mixture of sadness for the sick, old man and an insane desire to press him for more information. He'd known her mother. He would have known her father. Would he know why her father killed Celeste and then himself?

James eyes filled with tears as she squeezed his hand gently. "Hello James. Would you like to come and sit next to me?"

Blinking quickly he nodded, moved her hand to his arm and shuffled her in a clumsy walk to the head of the table, heading for a spot that was obviously his. He stopped next to a chair and pulled it out for her and then moved to his own. He stood, one hand resting on the back of his chair as he looked closely at her. "You do look like her," he said quietly, eyes suddenly seeming alert with comprehension.

Holly winked, ignoring the lurch in her belly. "I know."

Jack put a large bowls of fluffy rice and salad on the table next to the pot of beef stew and began ladling out a serving to his father. It looked delicious, and the meaty smell of the stew set her stomach to grumbling again. Jack looked up at the sound and laughed loudly. He nodded toward the dishes with a smile. "Help yourself, there's plenty."

She didn't need prompting twice. The strange little group enjoyed the meal in comfortable silence, little need for small talk as the good food and wine was savored. Finally Holly sat back in her chair with a satisfied smile, her plate scraped clean.

The pair chattered easily as they cleaned up after the meal; James snoozing on the couch in front of a TV blaring gospel music.

James leaned against the bench as he dried a plate Holly had just placed in the dish rack. He looked at her with a curious smile. "I'm itching to ask you a nosy question. I hope doesn't offend you," He said setting the dry plate on the bench and reaching for another.

Holly glanced sidelong at him and raised an eyebrow. "Hit me with it then."

"Why did you come back? I'm glad you did, but what drew you here after so long?"

Holly hands deep in the hot sudsy water stopped for a second as she scrubbed the last dish. She considered the question carefully. It was quite clear to her what she came back for when she decided to make the trip—to find out about her parents. As time went by, and during the long trip home it changed to a deeper need. To not only fill in the blanks of a life forgotten, but to find out where she was from as well.

"My parents I guess—to remember." She sighed and placed the last dish in the rack, squeezing out the dish cloth and wiping down the bench. "I lived in care for so long and heard the other kid's stories of where they were from, and I had none to give. I want that story I suppose."

"I could take you exploring if you like. Take you on a tour of the island?" He flicked his dish towel at her playfully. "It might take you down memory lane—or you could just get to see where you're from."

Holly smiled with pleasure. "Deal." Stealing his towel to dry her hands, she flicked him playfully back. "I'll go to the store tomorrow morning and stock up and then cook you dinner tomorrow night."

After checking James was still sleeping in front of his TV show, Jack offered to walk Holly home. Walking through the quiet roads home Holly shivered in the warm evening breeze. The scent of Queen of the Night blossoms filled the air, a perfume that carried a memory floating below the surface, tugging impatiently to be remembered.

"Cold?" Jack asked. He slid an arm around her and brought her close into his body as they walked, rubbing his hand up and down her arm.

She hadn't been, but now she was decisively warm, cheeks flushing with heat. His innocent touch had caused a jolt to her heart that had been quite unexpected. She was glad the night was dark, and the torches light the only illumination. She shook her head and squeaked out a non-committal reply, not trusting herself to get a whole sentence out without embarrassing herself.

Nearing the house Jack dropped his arm from around her shoulders, but grabbed her hand and swung it between them. He walked her up the steps to the porch and waited while she switched on the lights. They stood awkwardly and stared at each other for a moment, and then burst into laughter.

"I feel like we were on a date." Holly grinned. "All we need now is for my foster dad to yell something smart out the window."

"Or flash the lights to tell you to go inside," he said with a laugh. His eyes sparkled with humor as he stared down at her, and suddenly grew serious. "There is something that usually happens at the end of a date."

He bent and touched his lips gently to hers, mouth gentle but firm. Before she had time to react, kiss him back, or even breathe he squeezed her hand, gave her a naughty grin and bounced down the stairs.

As he disappeared into the dark, his torch light wobbling before him, he left a surprised and dazed Holly on the stoop. With a cheeky chuckle he called over his shoulder. "I'll see you about ten tomorrow!"

\* \* \* \*

Holly awoke early after a dreamless sleep, eager to start the day. Switching on the kettle for her morning coffee she leaned against the sink bench dreamily peeling an orange and popping the sweet segments into her mouth. She wasn't sure if she was keener to see the island, or to see Jack again. His kiss, no matter how fleeting, had sent alarm bells ringing, and now she could think of nothing but him.

Making her coffee and moving to sit out on the porch, she watched the sky lighten, and the town come alive. An ATV bike roared noisily past, wheels kicking up dust, the woman driving shooting her a surprised wave as she drove out of sight. Birds chirped a good morning in the sudden silence. She smiled happily as she sipped at her hot drink. Even writing didn't seem like such a chore as it had been in the last few months before coming to Pitcairn.

Walking to the store with a bounce in her step she was blind to the curious looks from locals as she passed the town square. The center of Adamstown held the Post Office, Government Treasury, Council Offices, and was open only three times a week. There was no call for opening more than that with such a small population. Most gathered here on those opening mornings not just to use the services but also to gossip and catch up on the town news. Little to her knowledge she was the prime and only news that morning.

Meanwhile in the tiny supermarket, just meters down the road from those gossiping in the Square, Holly picked out the ingredients for dinner that night, plus essentials to fill her cupboards.

At the counter she was greeted with a warm smile and a

friendly hello from a tall lanky woman tanned a nut brown from the sun. Short spiky blonde hair, blue eyes and a cheeky smile, she cheerfully welcomed her to the island and introduced herself as Kristy. "Come up for a coffee sometime. I'll introduce you to my boyfriend Marty. He's a Pitcairner, I'm not." She laughed raucously. "I'm a Quality Import from New Zealand." She leaned over the counter and whispered an aside. "I'm normal, unlike some of these other buggers." She giggled as she nodded her head in the direction of some of the other shoppers, "Though sometimes that's debatable."

Holly felt an immediate camaraderie with this woman and smiled happily at her. "Definitely. Sounds like fun."

Juggling three heavy plastic bags, Holly's good mood extended to the two elderly ladies enjoying the cool of the morning sitting on a bench just outside the store entrance.

"Good morning," she said with a smile, and then on a whim added, " Or should I say Wut-a-way?"

The older of the two women laughed loudly. "Yorley speak Pitkern?"

"No, not really," Holly said with a self-depreciating smile, laying her groceries at her feet. Once again heavy bags were cutting red marks into her fingers. Rubbing her hands together she smiled shyly at the women. "I only know how to say hello."

The woman converted to English so Holly could better understand them. The Pitkern language Holly knew was a mixture of English and Tahitian morphed into a sort of pigeon English. Easy to follow if the speaker spoke slow enough, hard if they spoke in the normal fast conversational tone.

"You're Celeste and Sammy's daughter?" the same woman asked.

"Yes—Holly."

"Well I'm Sarah and this here is Masie." She grinned. "You'll get to know us and Pitkern pretty quickly, there's not too many of us, and we all speak it." Sarah pointed to the bags at Holly's feet. "You'll need to get a bike at some point if you don't want to end up using walking everywhere—that is if you're staying?"

Here it is, that questioning look she'd been waiting for. Holly grinned. "I don't know yet. I am trying to figure out a few things. I only just found out about my parents."

Sarah and Masie exchanged looks. Masie finally broke her silence but directed a comment in Pitkern at Sarah so fast that Holly struggled to catch it. "Sammy either want to ride et, or be

William with et." The two women cackled loudly, leaving Holly bewildered, eyebrow raised. The comment was about her father, that she understood, but the rest sounded like gibberish to her uneducated ear.

Kristy popped her head around the door and caught Holly's eye. Shaking her head and flapping her hand toward the two old ladies with a 'never you mind' movement she mouthed, "Call me."

Nodding at Kristy and rolling her eyes, she picked up the bags and started the walk home, calling a curt goodbye to the still cackling women. She supposed she could have asked what they meant, but with Kristy's reaction to it—it could not have been nice. *I'll ask Jack later with no prying eyes or ears around,* she thought.

On her walk past the square she was not unaware of the stares from those gossiping in the center of town. Forcing a smile on her face she threw a hello in the general direction of the small group seated along the edges of the plaza, and hurried on, her good mood replaced with confused irritation.

# Chapter Three

Jack arrived right on time at ten o'clock as promised. He rumbled up the driveway riding a well-used ATV four wheeled quad, the bike farting and popping as it idled grumpily to a stop. With a bashful grin pasted over his face he met Holly at the door. "It sounds like a lemon, but gets me around."

Jack indicated for Holly to sit behind him on the bike. Bungee corded to the front carrier of the bike was a basket, cooler, and blanket promising the prospect of a picnic meal.

"I hope you haven't had a big breakfast."

"Just toast, why?"

"I've been cooking up a storm some good old Pitcairn cooking to fatten you up."

Holly laughed. "Oi, you saying I'm too skinny?"

Blushing, Jack smiled. "Definitely not." He helped her onto the bike and leered, twisting an imaginary villain's mustache. "You're delightful madam."

He slid onto the bike in front of her and keyed it into life, throwing a last comment over his shoulder, voice louder to fight the roar of the bike.

"Masie told me you need some meat on your bones—blame her."

He laughed and Holly wound her arms around his waist to hang on, the vibrations of his chuckle felt through his back to her chest.

Competing with the rumble of the bike, and the wind through their hair, Jack loudly kept up a running commentary as they drove along the winding roads.

Passing a signpost that said 'John Adams Grave', he said, "The only grave marked on Pitcairn for the mutineers is old John Adams. He's buried up there with his wife and child where the old Fletcher Christian homestead used to be."

Holly felt a pang of excitement, her good mood returning. The history of the island was infamous and she'd read with ferocious interest once she'd found out she herself could trace back to Fletcher Christian—the leader of one of the most famous seafaring Mutiny's ever.

She excitedly leaned forward to speak as he drove. "I can trace right back to Christian on my father's side, McCoy's on my mother's."

Jack nodded. "Most of us can. I've got Quintal in my direct line, and also the Warren's who married Pitcairners. They were sailors off whaling ships."

Holly mused how intertwined Pitcairners were and how rich their history was. Books she'd read had waxed lyrical about the romantic and brutal mutiny so long ago. Pitcairn Island was the hideaway of the Her Majesty's Armed Vessel Bounty and the crew who mutinied in 1790 against the dastardly Captain Bligh. Fletcher Christian had rallied the crew one night and set the Captain adrift in a longboat in the middle of the South Pacific. In a feat of seamanship never seen or heard of before Bligh sailed his loyal crew forty two days before reaching Timor without a compass or sextant.

Fletcher and eight more of his mutineer companions reached the recently discovered Pitcairn Island which had been chartered incorrectly on most mariners' maps of the day, and were never seen again. When the island was finally rediscovered only the descendants of Fletcher, his crew, and the Tahitian consorts lived there. Jack was proof of it, with extra bloodlines added to the gene pool from sailors off whaling ships and more recently immigrants added from New Zealand, Australia, and England.

The drive along the dusty roads ended far too soon for Holly. She hadn't forgotten the brief kiss Jack had surprised her with the night before and she'd been enjoying sitting so close behind him, the feel of her arms around his waist as she hung on. She hoped he didn't realize she'd not really felt the need to hold on so tight. She'd felt quite comfortable with his driving. She giggled to herself. She probably scared the poor guy with her clinginess.

They'd parked along a fern-lined track, the road petering out to a small seating area by a large overhanging rock. Helping her off the bike and shouldering the basket he pointed down a well-kept pathway. "We're heading down there." Passing her the blanket with a smile he grabbed the cooler and basket, then started off down the tree-lined track ahead of her.

Where are we going?" Holly asked as she hurried to keep up with his brisk pace. The track started to undulate and grow steeper and she watched as Jack, nimble as a goat, pick his way over the stony, rougher path. The tree's thinned out and the foliage on either side of the track became sparser, only stick-like bushes managing to grow from the cracks in the rock that now lined and made up the track.

"Christian's Cave. You're not afraid of heights are you?"

"No, I don't think so. The only heights I'm used to are high rise offices in Auckland though. Why?"

"That's why." Jack stopped and pointed. Holly shaded her eyes with her hand and looked up. Towering high above them set in a cliff face that would be a vertical climber's wet dream was a cave—more a notch in the cliff wall. "Fletcher used to sit and watch for ships up there."

"Oh, my, well, I guess we're going to find out pretty quickly if I'm height phobic," she said with a nervous laugh.

They continued round the last bend of the track and came to a rocky slope heading straight up toward the cliff face that led to the cave. Barren, steep, and imposing Holly paused for a moment to catch her breath, watching Jack as he pranced up the precipitous incline, loaded down with his basket and cooler. He made it seem easy, his breath not labored, muscles in his calves bunching and releasing as he made his way up the hill. Holly, carrying only the light fluffy blanket, puffed and blew like a steam train as she slogged her way up behind him.

He was waiting for her grinning widely as she finally—red faced and exhausted—made it to the cliff wall. He laughed and took the blanket as she put her hands on her knees and bent to catch her breath.

"Not much further, just around the bend and across a ledge. It'll be worth the walk."

Holly had to admit he wasn't wrong. Standing in the shallow cave after a short walk across a very narrow ledge carved into the cliff face, a drop of over one hundred and fifty feet ensuring her careful footing, the view was amazing.

Hands on her narrow hips, she looked out over Adamstown stretching out far below her in the valley, the ocean stretching far beyond that, the sky kissing the sea. Frigate birds and white Fairy Terns soared over the tree line, the roofs of houses shining silver bright with their tin coverings. The sheer beauty of it nearly brought her to tears.

Jack moved to stand beside her and slid an arm around her waist, his touch sending an electrical charge surging through her body. She stared out to the horizon stunned at her body's instant reaction to his simple embrace.

He gazed, blind to the reaction he'd caused her, out over the town, "Beautiful isn't it?"

She cleared her throat, scared that the tremor through her frame would translate to her voice. "Breathtaking. I can imagine Fletcher sitting up here, eyes on the horizon, watching for British Naval vessels."

She glanced back into the cave, or niche really. It was barely a dent in the cliff, she could walk 10 paces from where she was standing on the edge, and she'd be at the back wall. Looking up here from the road it had looked impressive and imposing. Up here it just looked small and claustrophobic.

"It used to have vines covering the entrance," Jack said. "According to the old people, Fletcher used to climb down from the cliff above on the vines and sit here to get away from everyone, and muse about the community."

Jack took her hand and squeezed it, smile twitching on his lips. "We'll have an early lunch and then head down Tedside to the rock pools." He paused and turned her to him, suddenly serious, brown eyes searching hers. "But first there's something I've wanted to do since I left last night."

He pulled her to him, slipping his hands behind the small of her back as she looked up into his face, locking in on the intense look in his deep brown eyes. Her heart skipped a beat and started racing out of control as she realized hazily that he was going to kiss her.

Her mind dully tried to override the clamor that her heart was making, asking annoyingly how could she been feeling this way after only one day. The sudden desire and attraction she felt for this stranger was madness. She could stop this now, pull away and control the moment, but the roaring of her heart drowned out the nagging voice in her head. This felt right, somehow this was meant to be, no matter how crazy it seemed.

As he bent his head to hers, she ran her hands up his arms, his lips touching hers as she brought her hands to the back of his head, their mouths at first tentative, lips moving, breath mingling. The kiss deepened and he pulled her hard against him, hands running up her back and into her hair, tongues meeting, tasting, lips hungry for more. Good sense told her to stop this insanity, but her ,traitorous deaf heart sent her back for more as she devoured the moment, pulling herself up on her toes to kiss him back, a moan escaping with an uncontrollable passion felt deep within her.

Jack pulled back, brown eyes darkened with passion. "I have to stop, things could get dangerous."

Drawing an unsteady breath Holly laughed shakily. "—falling off the cliff or did you have different intentions?"

Jack took her hand and led her to the blanket he'd spread on the cave floor. With a wicked smile, he said, "Both."

Holly covered the confusion she now felt with a smile. "You rouge."

Without his arms around her and his lips tempting, her mind cleared, her heart settled to a dull thump, she could think straight. She watched him numb, as he opened the basket and lay out some food, hunger and eating the last things on her mind.

*What the heck am I doing? Jack seems like a nice man, but my reaction to him is beyond ridiculous. This just doesn't happen in real life. You're not in some cheesy romance novel where the hero has the heroine in the sack five minutes after meeting. You're an idiot.* She shook her head as her mind chastised her heart.

As she watched him unpacking the picnic basket, her mind in a whirl, she noticed a scar flashing white on his elbow and a memory sizzled in her brain, flickering just out of reach.

Reaching out to trace the jagged white line on his skin with her finger, she couldn't shake the feeling of knowing how this happened. "How did you get this?"

He grinned, twisting to look at her. "You should know, you did it."

"I did?" Holly started in shock as the memory became crystal clear. A swing set behind the house, Jack, a freckle faced boy with a shaggy mop of brown hair. Poking out his tongue, screwing up his face, teasing her mercilessly, not letting her have a turn on her own swing, laughing at her when she yelled at him in a fit of temper.

"Get off, Jack! It's *my* turn!"

Her childhood voice echoed in her mind, chills shooting up and down her spine as she remembered, making her hug herself tight against the memory.

"Oh, God. I pushed you off the swing!"

"Yeah, and the swing came back and clonked me on the elbow. Five stitches it took to close it up."

She grimaced. She even remembered now the white bandage that graced his arm as he had showed her the damage she'd caused. "How can I remember that, and not my parents?"

He shrugged and with a smirk poked her gently in the side. "I'm just glad you remembered me finally."

"Yeah—that you were a pain in the bum and a tease."

Jack roared with laughter. "You used to call me a pain all the time."

Holly smiled, she remembered his laugh too; that hadn't changed either. With a jolt she realized she could remember a lot of things about him. How mad she used to get when he teased her. How he was always there if she fell or when she was upset. How she'd loved him. Her smile faded and she shook her head to clear her thoughts. This was going too fast. The emotions she was feeling right now just could not be trusted. Far too much was happening that she didn't comprehend.

"Jack."

He glanced at her and did a double take at her serious face. "What?"

"This is going to fast—us. Now...I just can't."

He stretched out a hand to stop her, his brow furrowed eyes saddened. "I understand. Doesn't mean I like it—but I understand." He smiled. "I'd still like to spend time with you though."

"I'd like that too."

"You're starting to remember aren't you?"

She nodded unable to look at him, scared he'd see the emotions running riot in her eyes. "I remember you."

He passed her a soda with a smile and waggled his eyebrows to catch her attention. "It's a good start. You've got the best part of Pitcairn in just that one memory."

Cracking up with laughter, thankful that the serious mood was broken, Holly relaxed a little and helped herself to a sandwich. Her appetite had reappeared with vengeance. She was suddenly starving. They lapsed into a comfortable silence while they ate, each in their own thoughts, Holly turning over the conversation in the store once again in her mind. Explaining to Jack what Masie had said to Sarah, she asked what they had meant.

Jack almost choked on a bite of his sandwich. Coughing and trying not to laugh at the same time, he beat on his chest with his closed fist. Eyebrows raised and eyes watering he spluttered with laughter, shaking his head. "Dirty old women."

With a smile he explained. "Ride in Pitkern means to have sex, and William means fight or you're grumpy, so what Masie said was that your dad either wanted to have sex with your mum, or fight with her." The smile disappeared from his face and he shot Holly an apologetic shrug. "Typical Masie. She opens her mouth and words just fall out before her mind clicks into gear. Sorry, it was insensitive of her."

"You didn't say it!" Holly cried. The comment as far as she knew was probably true enough. The consequences of her father being "William" was her mother being shot and killed she thought angrily. "I'm going to have to learn to speak Pitkern pretty quick aren't I?"

Jack smiled and pointed a finger, making a tick in the air. "Another reason to hang around with me!"

Holly popped the last of her sandwich in her mouth with a grin and chewed thoughtfully. She didn't think she needed any reason to justify hanging around with Jack. She felt drawn to him already.

The pair packed up their lunch leftovers and hiked back down from the cave, Holly getting to slow down this time and really appreciate the walk through the leafy track. This time she noticed the bird houses littering tree branches and posts, birds of all colors appreciating their man made homes. Name tags graced native plants, signs pointed out places of interest.

As promised they made the long ATV bike trek over the island to Tedside, Jack explaining the name had morphed from T'otherside—literally being the other side of the island from town.

No sandy white stretches of beach on this rocky volcanic isle of Pitcairn, but down here on this side of the island there was one small protected cove. The bay had a rocky shoreline that had trapped a smattering of coral white sand by a collection of shallow rock pools—as Jack explained, usually used when little kids learned to swim. For the first time a memory of the island itself returned to Holly, a happy moment playing in the pools, an adult sitting on the rocks behind her, dangling their bare legs into the water.

Holly stared with pleasure at Jack, the memory warming her heart. "I used to play in this pool when I was little!"

On impulse she rolled the legs of her cargo pants up higher around her taut thighs, kicked off her sandals and sat on the edge of a flat rock, dangling her legs into the salty water just as the adult did in her memory. The warm sea-water lapped around her calves, cold gushes of water invading the warmth as surf refreshed the pools in rhythmic waves.

Joining her on the rock, Jack smiled. "We all did when we were kids." He laughed. "Now, we come down, light a fire and cook sausages over the hot coals and enjoy a beer or three."

Holly smiled at the thought. Shooting Jack a sidelong glance, she smiled shyly. "Thanks for today, Jack." Over a few short hours she'd not only filled a blank space in her memory, but added a jig-saw section of a piece missing from her heart.

# Chapter Four

Jack whistled happily as he entered the house and closed the door with a jaunty back kick. He'd just dropped of Holly at her place and was already looking forward to seeing her again tonight for dinner. The moment he'd seen her yesterday morning something had changed in his life. It was as if he'd been holding his breath for years, the sight of her finally reminding him to exhale. *Whew,* he thought, *I feel like she's hit me over the head with a brick. I can hardly think straight.*

With a bounce in his step he walked down the hall into the kitchen where he dumped the picnic basket and cooler on the bench. The house was silent and empty. The quiet was a bit unnerving. Usually at this time of day Dad and Masie would be nattering, ensconced in their favorite chairs in the lounge. "Masie? Dad?"

"Out here, Jack!" Masie called from the garden out the back.

Emerging onto the sun drenched back porch, he found the two busy podding wild beans, splitting the strong smelling pods with their fingernails, and scooping the tasty green beans out into a large ceramic bowl, discarding the pods into scrap buckets for the chickens. Masie's aged, lined hands worked quickly, splitting and discarding three or four pods to James' one.

Jack pulled up another chair next to his father and pulled the half-full basket of un-podded beans over. This was a time consuming chore he hated, but loved the resulting dinner accompaniment. *Wild beans with coconut milk—yum!* He thought as his belly yowled agreement. *I'll take some over with us to Holly's tonight.*

"Mekin' beans for you'se dinner, ain't we James?" Masie said with a smile, patting James age-spotted hand maternally. James nodded and grunted assent, eyes never leaving the pod he was attempting with great difficulty to open, his hands shaking with the effort to get the small bean to crack open.

"Thanks Masie, I'll cook some up for him tonight. We're going out, so at least I'll have something to take with us."

Masie's eyebrows disappeared into her hairline. Her mouth opening ready to make a smart reply, but James cut her off before she got a chance. He eyed his son with a frown, brow creasing.

"Where've you been, Son? Your mum's been worried. You better go tell her you're home."

Masie tut-tutted and rolled her eyes. "I told you James. He's been out with that girl." She threw an empty pod into the chicken bucket with disgust. "Jack's a grown man, he bin out courting ha gal for Sammy's, James."

Grunting, James sat back in his chair, staring with confusion at Masie. "I es know Jack's grown, yous foolish woman." He shot Jack a sidelong glance and then looked at his hands, muttering. "Damn woman thinks I es know nothing."

Jack shot Masie a furious look, his mouth pursed into a tight frown. "Masie, *that* gal is Holly. Not Celeste's gal, Sammy's gal, or my gal. Holly."

He picked up another lot of un-podded beans, dumping them in his lap, and beginning to pod them as if on automatic pilot, the heat of her frown burning a hole in his forehead. He looked up and cleared his throat to give himself a second to think. *This needed to be clear, so she didn't misunderstand—she wasn't going to like it, but it had to be said.* "You can cut out the town gossip around her too."

Masie looked at him, eyes wide with hurt, hands stilled. "I'm sure I don't know *what* you mean." She threw the half worked bean pod back in the basket with an insulted sniff, her face screwing up into an expression of distaste. "If you're going to be like that I'll go home, thank you *very* much."

Jack sighed with exasperation. *He knew she'd take it the wrong way.* It didn't bode well to upset the people who helped him look out for his Dad. *The old woman was always here for the old fulla,* he thought. *Masie was a tough old bird, tongue sharp as a knife, but she meant well—*he hoped.

"Sorry, Masie...but, please be nice. She's one of us you know."

Mollified, Masie relaxed in her chair and began shucking the beans again. "She's been gone a long time though Jack." She poked a bean in his direction. "She may not stay either. Don't get your knickers in a twist over her."

Jack rolled his eyes. *Wasn't worth the argument to even try and discuss it with her. Time to change the subject.*

"How was Dad today?"

"Good. Well, he's been talking about Celeste a lot. Dunno if that's a good thing Jack. It upsets him." She looked at him sidelong. "You know es cause Holly's back, she reminds him of Celeste.

Spitting image of her mother—even I es see et. Don't blame the old fella."

James grunted, his eyebrows knitting together as he frowned at Masie. "Stop talking about me like I'm five years old."

He looked up at Jack, a sparkle of the old intelligence in his eyes Jack had not seen for a long time, a smile on his gnarled face. "Holly's a good girl. I like her." His eyes grew hazy, the light of recognition waned, awareness left his face, cheeks slackening. "You two just play close to home. Your mum worries."

Jack smiled sadly, the glimpse of his 'old' father too short. These episodes were becoming far and few between these days. "Okay, Dad." He leaned over and gave him a one handed hug, heart breaking a little as he realized how much he was losing, as his father suffered through this cruel disease.

"We're going over to see Holly for dinner tonight."

Masie snorted, snide smile tugging at her lips. "Har girl was always following you 'bout when you was little, and she following you 'bout like a bad smell now. Nothing's changed."

James fixed Masie with a fierce look. "You leave 'em kids alone."

He threw his mangled bean in the basket in frustration. "I'm tired of these damn beans. Pah. Women's work," he growled.

Masie smiled at Jack victoriously. "See, you've worn the old man out with you's chatter about ha girl."

She rose queen-like to her feet and strode over to Jack's father imperiously, putting a hand under his elbow. "Come on James; we'll go put you some Gospel on the TV."

As Masie escorted her father inside Jack shook his head, laughed to himself and continued shucking. Masie was a pain in the arse, but she kept life interesting, and she'd never let him down with his father. If he could only get her off Holly's back, life would be perfect.

The thought of Holly brought a smile to his lips and his fingers stuttered in their work with the beans. He was curious about the attraction that throbbed between them—it was mutual. He knew *that* after kissing her this morning. He'd never wanted to kiss someone as badly as he had wanted to kiss her this morning. It was as if he was magnetically drawn to her. It was crazy really. She was right, he supposed, to want to slow it done some. One day back on island and he was all over her. He cringed a little inside, thinking about how forward he was.

After twenty odd years apart, it seemed to him, as if she'd never left, that their friendship had just continued over from the day she'd been taken away. He remembered that violently emotional day well—too well. If painful memories left welts, it would have left a doozy. He shook his head to rid himself of the thought. He didn't want to think about it. It was something he'd have to talk to Holly about at some point though; he knew it would be a question she'd want answered.

When she'd opened the door to his knock yesterday he'd been surprised, shocked. It wasn't that she looked different. That she'd grown up—so had he. It wasn't the physical thing. He grinned—of course it was the physical thing—she was gorgeous, all blond hair, green eyes, and legs that just wouldn't quit. His grin widened as his mind betrayed him with a very lecherous thought about those legs wrapping around...*Down boy*, he chided himself with a laugh.

There was some sort of *connection* between them though. He'd always felt like something was missing. Seeing her again yesterday made him feel like it was found. *How dorky*, he snickered, as he gave up on the beans. He wasn't in the mood for the tedious task.

*I'd rather daydream of something much more pleasant.*

Masie found him legs outstretched, feet resting on her chair, arms behind his head, lost in thought. "Hoi you lazy bugger." She swatted his feet off her chair and sat down heavily, reaching for the basket he'd abandoned.

"You's dads nodding off in front of the TV. Let him rest till yorley drag him off to you's gal." Her nimble fingers resumed podding the beans, her mouth set in a firm line. "It's not you's father's fault you know."

Jack stared, waited for the rest. She continued working, eyes downcast intent on her chore, but her wrinkled cheeks were a deep pink betraying her emotions.

"What's not Dad's fault?"

"What happened with Sammy an' Celeste." Masie's chin sunk into her chest in her endeavor not to look Jack straight in the eye. "Ha gal of Sammy's, she was trouble. Yorley's father was just part of her plan. She used him to get what she wanted."

Jack's blood boiled, he knew exactly what she was insinuating—that his dad had an affair with Celeste. He'd heard all this nasty gossip before. It royally pissed him off, he thought, fighting to stop himself from grinding his teeth in annoyance. People here talked without thinking, ignorant of the consequences of such vicious prattle.

He was young when Samuel shot Celeste, but he wasn't stupid.

The antics between a man and a woman—although slightly icky to his young mind, then—were not something he was blind to. He remembered his mum and dad canoodling in the kitchen, kissing and cuddling—they were always doing it. It made him roll his eyes and tell them they were gross, but it also made him feel safe, that he was in a loving family.

That was the reason that the gossip he'd heard before, about his father and Celeste had just rolled of his back like rain off a slicker. The affection his parents showed to each other, even after five kids and a long eventful marriage, didn't indicate to him in any way, shape or form a chance of adultery. He'd know wouldn't he? He lived with the guy for just under thirty years, for heaven's sake, he'd have known if his father was off jiggy jigging with the next door neighbor. No, nope, just wasn't possible.

Jack sat forward and spoke in a voice that left Masie no doubt that he was serious. "Masie? I appreciate all you do for Dad, but what you're insinuating is just plain bull. It's hurtful, untrue and based on gossip that was half baked twenty years ago and is worse now. Cut. It. Out."

Masie's face colored a deep purple, her lips pressed so firmly together they almost disappeared off her face into her mouth. She shook a finger angrily in his face.

"I know what I know young man. You were too young to see it, but I wasn't."

No longer afraid to look into his eyes, she glared at Jack, mouth spitting venomous words.

"Har gal hung round yorleys father like a bad smell, I saw et, yous mother saw et and so did Sammy. Why do you think yous parents nor tek Holly? Your father beg yous mother fer tek ha gal. Why do yorley think they sent ha girl away to New Zealand? Open yous eyes boy."

Jack recoiled back into his chair with shock, mouth dropping open in horror. He refused to believe her vitriolic words, it couldn't be true.

Masie's face crumpled, eyes filling with crocodile tears as she reached forward and patted his knee to comfort him. Her eyes, though teary, held triumph, pleasure in the pain she'd so obviously caused.

"I nor mean to upset yorley. The truth mean to come out sooner or later."

Jack saw red. Enough was enough. Standing up with as much dignity as he could—considering he wanted to take the chair he vacated and smack her with it—he glared down at the sadistic woman.

"Who's truth? Yours? I don't think so."

Leaning down and looking right into her face, he stared with steely determination into her eyes. Masie shrunk back into her chair, phony tears drying in her eyes.

"I hear you've upset Holly with any of this nonsense, help or no help, you'll not step foot in this house again."

Walking away before he completely snapped and wrung the woman's neck, Jack struggled internally with her words. No matter how much he wanted to ignore them as pure lies and innuendo, something had struck true. He only hoped Holly didn't catch wind of this before he got to the bottom of it first.

Jack checked on his father. He'd as usual, turned up the volume on the TV to deafening levels; and was fast asleep, his snores loudly competing with the gospel music. Stretched out in his favorite chair, mouth sagging open, drool pooling at the corner of his mouth, James looked a shadow of the man Jack remembered.

Heavy footsteps marched down the hall, and the front door slammed, vehemently signaling Masie's huffy departure as she stomped off down the porch. *Good riddance* he thought with uncharitable grumpiness.

*Shit.* He stuck his hands on his hips and looked down at the floor, regretting his words even though he'd meant every one. He should go after her and just make sure he hadn't pissed her off too much. He hated the lecturing, constant interference and meddling, but she still was there every day for Dad. *Why do you have to confuse me so much. Say such horrible things. What do you know about my father I don't?*

Jack sunk down into the chair opposite his father and stared blindly. Raking his fingers through his hair, he dropped his head down into his hands. *What the hell did you do Dad? What the hell did you do?*

# Chapter Five

The early morning sun streamed through the curtain-less windows. Holly stretched catlike in her bed, the fresh, white sheets tangling in her legs with her movement. *Must remember to put those drapes up,* she thought drowsily. Checking her watch with a yawn she noticed it was only just past seven.

She felt lazy and decadent lying in this late, but to her surprise she didn't care. She was usually up much earlier than this in New Zealand, either writing, or getting ready for work, but she knew here there was no pressure for either—well, until her royalty savings dried up anyway. She had enough squirreled away to last, if she lived frugally, for at least a few months

Debating whether to get out of bed or to just lay and enjoy the morning sunlight was as much as she could deal with at the moment. The evening before had been a strange and uncomfortable occasion, with Jack subdued and James having a bad night, constantly mistaking her for her mother, and then becoming upset being out of his usual surroundings.

The trio had eaten a quick meal, Holly hardly tasting the food she'd spent all afternoon slaving over. As soon as they'd risen from the table, Jack had begged her forgiveness and taken James home. Jack had kissed her briefly good night and promised to see her in the next few days, but he'd been distant, distracted.

She could understand Jack wanting to take his sick father home, but, selfishly she wondered if she'd upset Jack yesterday asking him to slow things down. If she were honest with herself, she was disappointed with his lack of affection. He hadn't so much as attempted to hold her hand.

Holly sprawled on the bed, laughing at her own arrogance. Push the guy away, then get pissed off because he did exactly as she'd asked. She rolled over and pressed her face into the pillow. *Make up your mind you contrary woman.* Holly thumped the bed with her fist. *That's enough self-centered thinking for today, get up you lazy bones!*

Throwing off the covers she climbed out of bed and dressed—shorts and a light T-shirt to fight the heat of the day. There was no way she was going to lie in bed and rue what she couldn't change.

She had traveled the self-pity train for too long in New Zealand when she first discovered her past.

Toothbrush in her mouth, she brushed her teeth as she walked through the house, switching on the kettle and her computer, then wandered back down to the bathroom. Still berating herself for being so contrary she rinsed her brush and stuck it back in the toothbrush holder, splashed cold water on her face and then leaned on the bathroom sink and stared at herself in the mirror. She smiled at the idiot reflected back at her. "Make up your mind what you want dummy." The idiot grinned wider at the insult and Holly dissolved into giggles.

Pouring her coffee and sitting down at the kitchen table she faced her computer. Pulling her long hair back into a loose pony-tail she logged on and then flicked up the Internet. Checking emails and finding a reply from Rosy, she read the news from home, not without a little pang of homesickness. She wrote a long winded, detail filled email back describing everything that had happened in the last few days, but purposely left out mentioning Jack. *That would take a lot longer to explain*, she thought smiling, *although Rosy would have loved news this juicy.*

Opening a new Word document she sat contemplating the blank screen, cursor flashing. The old dread threatened to rise, but she pushed it down with a firm resolve. *No stress, just think.* Leaning back in her chair she clutched her coffee, blowing over the top of the steaming cup, eyes glazing over as she looked blankly out the window.

Her coffee had cooled, still clutched in both hands before she took a mouthful, grimaced at the lukewarm sip, and put the cup to the side of the computer. Her fingers, at first tentative, moved across the keyboard as words began to flow, then flew in a blur as thoughts and words, fighting to beat the other to the page, translated to the screen.

Hours later she was astonished to find she'd written over seven pages, and still had more words itching to escape into the story. Coffee stone cold now, she rose to make another when a female voice called out with a loud "Whoo-hooo? Anyone home?" from the porch outside.

*Dammit*, she thought, *who the hell is that? I was on a roll!* Dashing back to the computer she hit save and closed the lid on the laptop.

"Yeah, in the kitchen! Come in." Holly called back.

Kristy walked into the kitchen just as Holly flicked on the

kettle. Holly waggled a cup with a grin. "Coffee?" *Now, Kristy was someone she didn't mind interrupting a roll,* she thought with a giggle, especially when Holly caught sight of what Kristy was carrying.

Kristy slid the tray of decadent looking chocolate cake onto the counter. With an overdone sigh of relief she grinned at Holly. "You should of seen me trying to drive and carry that thing. It wasn't pretty, let me tell you."

"I'd hate to think. Just glad I wasn't on the road with you," Holly said, with a laugh.

Kristy grinned. "Most people wish they weren't on the road with me—full stop."

Gathering together coffee items, forks and a knife, plates and napkins and placing them on the table, Holly pushed the computer out of the way. *She could write later,* she rationalized, *she missed her sister, and Kristy's happy-go-lucky attitude reminded her so much of Rosy it hurt.*

Slicing into the rich looking, dark cake, liberally drizzled with chocolate icing, Holly's mouth started to water. "Geez, I'm going to have to start walking every day if you make this a habit."

"The way I hear it, you're getting all the exercise you need," Kristy said, with a wink and a leering stare.

"Oh, good God. What have I done now?" Holly asked, mouth dropping open as she stared at Kristy in surprise. She shook her head. She'd heard the Pitcairn grapevine was bad, but this was ridiculous. She passed Kristy a plate with a slice of cake and poured her a coffee with a frustrated air. "Jesus, I've only been here five minutes."

Kristy grinned. "You're the new headline in town." She shrugged. "One, you're this mysterious Pitcairner returning home, and two, you've got Jack looking at you with big puppy dog eyes."

With the thought of Jack looking at her with puppy dog eyes dancing in her mind's eye, her stomach clutched into a tight ball, warmth spreading through her lower limbs.

Holly blushed furiously, and Kristy roared with laughter. "Oh my, you like him too."

Kristy shoved a forkful of cake into her mouth and rolled her eyes in ecstasy. "Oh God this is good, even if I do say so myself." She gestured with her cake fork as she spoke. "Don't let the bloody gossip get you down. I shouldn't have said anything. It was just funny listening to the old biddy's getting their knickers in a twist.

I will do some gossiping of my own though." Kristy leaned forward in her chair, pushed her plate out of the way and folded her arms on the table.

"Masie's pissed because Jack told her to mind her own business." She cackled with glee. "About time the old bag got her hand smacked. She's the biggest trouble-maker we've got, considering there are only seventy odd of us on island. She's the queen of uh-oh."

Holly smiled uncertainly. She didn't want any more issues on her plate than she already had, the whole town talking about her wasn't going to help her fit in to the insulated community at all, or for that matter get the answers that she wanted.

"I wonder who's business she was knee deep in—mine or his?" Holly's face twisted into a grimace.

"Probably both." Kristy smiled and reached out to pat Holly's hand. "Don't worry, you're only flavor of the month until some other poor fool does something interesting—or stupid." She laughed and took a sip of her coffee. "Usually I'm the fool—you're taking the heat off me for a change. Thanks!"

Holly grinned. "No problem, but please hurry up and do something idiotic fast, just to get me out of the spotlight. It's starting to get a bit warm."

Kristy played with the handle of her coffee cup and stared with open curiosity at Holly. "So what *is* going on with Jack?" She put her hand up as if stopping traffic. "Only asking for the sake of my own nosiness, so you can tell me to bugger off if you want."

Holly smiled at her directness. She didn't mind the question at all. It was better than being talked about behind her back. She toyed with the fork in her now empty cake plate as she contemplated the answer.

"I don't know. I couldn't remember a lot from my childhood, still can't. Jack though…"Pausing she shrugged. "Jack, I remember. When I'm around him it feels as if we've never been apart. It's weird, unnerving and…comfortable. Then, there are all these feelings he's stirring up piled on top of that."

"Jack's a sweetie. You couldn't find a nicer guy on the island." She waved a hand in the air with a grin. "Apart from Marty of course. Jack's been alone for a while. He was in New Zealand for a couple of years, studying engineering. I heard he had a steady girl out there, but she didn't want to give up the cushy life for a piddly little island in the middle of nowhere. Ever since he got home and James was diagnosed with Alzheimer's it's been tough."

Kristy put another sliver of cake into her mouth and chewed, a shrewd gleam in her eye as she considered Holly closely. "Jack seems happier these last few days. Even Marty noticed it."

She looked at Kristy shyly from under her eyelashes and smiled. "He kissed me yesterday. Made my toes curl."

Kristy burst into laughter and crossed her hands across her heart, swooning melodramatically. "Whoo, the guy works fast!"

"Mmm. I didn't stop him." She smiled inwardly. She'd just about pushed him off the edge of the cliff, she'd been so enthusiastic about kissing him back. "I did tell him afterward that we needed to slow it down a bit." She bit her lip, frown creasing her brow. "I think I might have blown it though, Jack and James came over last night for dinner and Jack was real quiet. Poor James was having a bad night. He was calling me Celeste, and getting really confused."

Kristy shook her head, screwing her mouth into a frown. "Yeah, I heard James had a bad day yesterday. His condition seems to get better, just before it gets worse." She paused. "Ya know, it's nice you had them over. They don't get out much. Jack especially. Some Friday nights he comes up for a game of darts, but mostly he's at home with his father. It would have been good for James to get out too." Kristy smiled. "You're good for them, you know."

Kristy pulled her plate back in front of her and scooped up a morsel of icing with a finger, licking it off. "I've worked with the elderly before. There's a term called 'sundowning'. Patients suffering Alzheimer's tend to worsen as the sun goes down. Sounds like maybe that's what James was going through. Jack might have been quiet worrying about his father."

"Ugh. Now I feel bad for worrying about my own trifling issues. I should have realized." Holly rolled her eyes at her own insensitivity. Reprimanding herself for being so selfish, she decided to walk over later to visit with James and see if Jack needed a break.

"Your issues aren't trifling, just different. You came back to find out about your parents right? That's a biggie considering the circumstances on why you left." Kristy stared at her with concern written across her face. "What are your plans? For getting the information you need, I mean."

Holly sighed. "I have no freaking idea. The amount of people here who knew my parents, only want to gossip about them, not tell me why they ended up as they did." She squirmed in her chair.

"So, how did *you* end up here?" Holly asked. She had done quite enough moaning about her own troubles she thought grimly. She was curious as to why Kristy, a born and bred New Zealander, had made the huge decision to live on an Island thousands of miles away from family and friends. It had to take a strong woman to make that move alone. *In my situation, I have a home and a questionable past to drag me back.*

"Came up for a six month rat eradication program on Henderson Island, met Marty and fell in love. Usual story." She grinned, her blue eyes twinkling. "Who wouldn't fall for me?" She aped primping an imaginary bouffant hairstyle and dissolved into laughter.

"Marty's gorgeous—a big teddy bear with a heart of gold—wait till you meet him. Just couldn't help myself falling for the big lug." She gazed dreamily past Holly, elbow on the table, hand supporting her chin. "I actually left him and went back to New Zealand after the project. I was home for about three months before I realized I couldn't just forget him and move on with my life. So, I moved my life here." Kristy smiled toothily. "Never regretted it, best thing I ever did. Apart from being with the man I love, the island grows on you—gets under your skin."

Holly wondered if she'd be feeling the same way Kristy did about the island, a few weeks or months down the track. Not even here a week and she was already perplexed over how people treated each other. *Kristy was one of the few 'normal' ones here*, she thought with a grin.

"Hey, I have to ask while I'm thinking about it. When I arrived here the other day there was bread, fruit, and the basics in the fridge, but no one's admitted to leaving them. I want to thank someone, but it's like the goodness fairy left it and disappeared." Holly was truly frustrated. She'd asked Jack last night if he'd managed to find out who it was and he'd had no idea. She didn't want to seem ungrateful and the food had been a godsend.

"Pitcairners are good that way; it's that sense of small town community. You just repay in kind. If you've got extra vegetables from the garden, you share." Kristy shrugged apologetically. "I wish I could help with a name, but it could be any of the locals. It's a throwback from when the island was even more isolated than it is now. You looked out for your neighbors, they looked out for you."

"There have been some hard times on the island lately. Lots of oldies, the young ones are leaving to find jobs and better lives elsewhere. Money's tight, the island's on budgetary aid, and people are struggling. That good neighbor ethic is what's getting a lot of people through."

"I didn't realize things were that bad."

"Yeah, the outside looks in and assumes it's an island paradise—and it is—no nine to five grind for us. We still have to live, the costs for petrol, power, phone, and all the normal 'outside' stuff still applies here, and at twice, sometimes three times the cost. We all have a government job of some sort. I work at the store for example and I'm a road worker, but without Marty's job as an engineer and tractor driver, we just wouldn't survive.

A thousand dollars of bills and debt a month, plus store bills, and getting one thousand five hundred in pay a month to cover it—well, we struggle. The pensioners are in a worse bind financially, not to mention the two families with kids, so I usually try not to complain as much as I am right now." Kristy laughed and shrugged. "I still wouldn't live anywhere else."

"How are people getting by then?" Holly couldn't understand how someone could live on so little. "Just my freight costs for my luggage almost ran me broke." She added.

"Gardens for fresh vegetables. Fish, either caught off the rocks, or off the boats. Trade with each other for spare parts for bikes, or bread. We do what we have to. Plus, if you know a pensioner is struggling you help I if you can get past them swearing black and blue they're fine without you nosing about in their affairs." Kristy laughed.

Holly sipped at her coffee, thinking about how lucky she actually was being financially secure, at least for now. "I've got a few months to decide what I'm going to do, then it's either look for a job here or go home. I've got family back there, and a job I can go back to."

Kristy tipped her head to the side, a questioning look on her face. "I thought you were here to stay."

Holly shook her head and sighed. "I have no idea what I want. I know I need to find out what happened to my parents—after that, who knows." She smiled at Kristy, who looked disappointed, shoulders drooping, mouth turning down. "Pitcairn may grow on me too."

"I hope so. It's nice having someone my age around. I hope you stay."

"Well, until the money runs out or they deport me, I'm here for a while."

Kristy snorted with laughter. "I'm sure I'm on the deportation list way higher than you! As for jobs—just depends what you want to do. Do you want to get your hands dirty? There are road jobs, or grounds work, like the lawns around government buildings. Or work in an office?"

"Either, or—doesn't matter really. If I can write from home as well...anything suits me."

Holly was surprised when Kristy got up to leave. The day had flown past, morning had turned into late afternoon and half the cake had disappeared, much to her chagrin. She really would have to start walking at this rate.

"Thanks for dropping in today, Kristy. You remind me of my sister, Rosy. I'll have to con her into coming up for a visit; you'll love her!"

Kristy laughed as she carried her empty coffee mug and plate to the kitchen sink. "Oh God, a good old girly get together. I need more of that please. Even better if we could con the government into building a mega-mall with a Starbucks. You think they'd fall for that?"

She made a firm friend on the island. Holly hugged her warmly, laughing at the twinkle in Kristy's eye as she mentioned a mall and coffee house. "I'd be happy if they'd just provide the mall." Holly covered the cake with plastic wrap and passed it to Kristy holding her belly, aching with sugar overload. "Next time leave the cake behind."

Kristy left laughing, but not before insisting Holly join her and Marty on Friday night. "We usually have a darts and pool night. Marty has his..." Kristy made imaginary quotation marks in the air with her fingers. "*Man Cave*. We have a few drinks and a few laughs." She grinned, and with a cheeky wink added, "Jack usually comes over for a while too."

Holly was still smiling as she closed the door behind Kristy who departed with a cheery wave. "See you Friday!"

# Chapter Six

Holly let herself out of the house and walked the short distance to Jack's feeling jumpy and inexplicably nervous. After such a productive morning at the computer and the brilliant afternoon spent with Kristy, she was confused by her sudden shift in mood. She was unsure what caused her the most panic, seeing Jack again, or bumping into Masie. "Pull yourself together woman," she muttered.

The covered area next to the house where Jack parked his bike was empty and she wavered at the beginning of the driveway racked with indecision. *Should I go in?* Holly laughed at her hesitancy. *Well at least I know Jack's not the one I'm anxious about having to face. I still feel as though I want to run away like a little girl.*

Irritated, she strode up onto the porch and knocked on the door. Voices buzzed inside before the sound of heavy footsteps approached. Masie opened the door wide, the look on her face changing suddenly from a welcoming smile, to a surprised, blank look.

"Oh, hello." Masie stood firmly in the middle of the doorway, expression morphing into a disapproving frown. "Jack's nor home. He's workin'."

Holly nodded and smiled, fighting the instant dislike that gnawed at her belly. "I saw his bike was gone. I came to visit with you and James." She hoped her little, white lie wouldn't backfire. She'd have preferred Masie wasn't there at all.

Masie reluctantly stepped back out of the doorway to let her pass. Pointing through to the lounge she snorted with disbelief. "James is in there. Don't upset him. He's having a good day for a change."

Slamming the door behind Holly hard enough to make the door jamb rattle, she stomped off down the hall. "I'll go put the kettle on. I s'pose you'll want some biscuits too." Without waiting for an answer, she disappeared into the kitchen straight-backed with disapproval.

Holly wandered into the lounge, heart suddenly racing in her chest, finding it hard to breathe in the cloying warmth of the stuffy room. Windows were shut tight, adding to the claustrophobic atmosphere. The room felt super-heated in the hottest period of the day, and Holly stumbled to a window, shoving it open against a sudden rush of dizziness, black spots swirling in front of her eyes.

Taking deep breaths of the fresh air that swirled around her and slightly cooled the room behind her, she turned back. Overstuffed couches, a large, new wide screen TV, bookcases, stuffed with hundreds of well-thumbed books, and displays of old Pitcairn, curio, and a large recliner cluttered the room.

Holly willed herself not to panic even as dread filled her every pore, the open window, the breeze, no excuse for the chill she now felt. An unexplainable sadness weighed down on her, threatening to crush her where she stood. James sat in the recliner, blanket spread across his knee, watching her carefully, curiosity and concern etched into his craggy face.

"You alright love?" he asked sitting forward in his chair, his hands gripping tight, the arms of his chair.

Holly gritted her teeth and nodded at James with a smile she hoped didn't look as forced as it felt. She strode across the room and collapsed into a chair opposite him. Rubbing a hand across her forehead she felt anything but normal—her mind descending into a black hole of remembrance.

Memories had come rushing back, flashes of darkness and light, like an old motion picture playing on a patchy movie screen.

An adult physically pulled her out of a man's arms-*James arms*. Her child-like voice screamed with the pain of loss, confusion and heartache. She had been wrenched from *this* house, *this* room.

She could remember Jack crying into his mother's skirts, James shouting, "It's not right I tell you! It's not right!" Jack's tear stained voice, calling her name as she was dragged, kicking and screaming down the drive, wrist locked in the firm grasp of an out of focus adult's hand.

Holly looked at James in shock as the memories settled into shattered pieces piercing her with their fragility. *What did James have to do with her past?* He stared back, mouth hanging open in concern. "Are you okay, Holly? You're as white as a ghost. Do you want me to call Masie?"

She shook her head. "No, no, I'm okay—just a headache." Masie's disapproval was all she needed right now. "It's the heat. I'm not used to it yet."

She struggled to set the world straight as reverberations of the memories echoed in her mind. She fought to tamp the emotions welling up within her, irritation surging below the surface. The more she remembered the more confused she became. *Why could she not remember everything?* Angry tears itched at the back of her eyes and threatened to overflow. With a lump in her throat, she cleared noisily, Holly fought to control herself in front of the old man.

James, mollified by her answer, sat back in his chair. "The heat gets all the new people." He laughed. "The mosquito's too—new blood!"

Nice of you to come visit, Holly. I don't get many visitors these days."

Masie stomped in carrying a loaded tray, sniffing her displeasure, mouth turned down at the corners in a disagreeable frown. "Well, I guess I don't count then." She placed the tray on the coffee table hard enough to make the cups rattle in their saucers, spoons clattering. "I'm just the hired help I suppose."

James laughed and cheekily patted her on her ample bottom. She stood next to him, arms folded across her heaving chest. "Well, you would be if I paid you, Masie, my dear. You're just help to me."

Holly, despite the turmoil still raging within her, surprised herself by laughing out loud. Masie's mouth twitched, a smile on the verge of escape. "Yous a cheeky ole' bugger James Quintal. Yorley should be grateful I turn up ya every day."

To Holly's amusement Masie's lined face had flushed pink with pleasure, an inkling of a smile quickly hidden as she bent to pour the refreshments, putting a small plate of chocolate covered biscuits where James could reach it easily.

James accepted the cup of tea Masie passed him with a gnarled and shaking hand, the dainty cup and saucer looking oddly delicate in his large fingers, and nodded at Holly. "So, tell me young lady, how are you enjoying being back home?"

"Everyone's asking me that." She accepted a cup from Masie with the heady scent of lemons merging with the bitter aroma of the black tea. "Jack's taken me on a quick tour, and I've met only a handful of the locals. The island is beautiful though. I'll have to do some more exploring."

Holly could hardly focus on the banal conversation that fell out of her mouth. She must have said the right things however, as James nodded and smiled.

She wished she could get James alone so she could ask him

the questions running through her brain like a breaking-news banner on an all news channel. She had remembered a revelation of separation—obviously after her parent's death. It had to be. The memory held pain, loss, desolation. James had been devastated to have her ripped from his arms, she'd been screaming to go back into the safety of his embrace. She'd felt safe there. She clung to that thought. Had James been fighting to keep her from foster care? The idea shook her to the core. Now more than ever she needed answers.

There was little chance though of a quiet conversation with James in this period of clarity he was enjoying. Masie had made herself at home, burrowing deep into one of the over-stuffed chairs. James's self-appointed chaperone, to ensure Holly kept in line and did not upset him.

Masie's previous sweet, smiling demeanor was well hidden now, as she sat slightly out of James eye-line, and glared with gleeful malevolence at Holly.

Ignoring the woman's baleful stare, Holly sipped at her tea. James reached for a biscuit, and chewed on it thoughtfully. "Are you still writing? We've been following you over the years, proud as punch. They've got two of your novels in the library."

Holly's eyebrows shot into her hairline in surprise.

"You've read my books? They're here on island?"

"Of course." He looked puzzled. "You're a Pitcairner, of course the library would stock your books. The last person who wrote a book here was Rosalind McCoy—and that was about the Mutiny and life after they settled on the island. Yours..."

James sighed dramatically. "Love, hate, the outside world, strong manly men, and the women with the strength to control them." He paused. "Brilliant."

They'd known about her! Shock left her speechless for a moment...all the time Masie needed to roll her eyes in distaste. Brows knitting together with a look of incredulity at James, the old woman spluttered. "Some people es proud, others think es waste of a people's time."

James snorted with frustration, turning his head back to glare at Masie. "Woman! Just because she ain't digging in a garden or baking a bread, et nor mean et's not work." Returning his attention to Holly, eyes softening, he leaned forward, cup tipping alarmingly in its saucer, tea slopping over the rim. "Your mum wrote too you know."

"She did?" Holly's mouth dropped open in surprise and she

leaned forward, matching James posture, eager to hear more about her mother. This was something they had in common, maybe where Holly's love of the written word had come from.

"She was always scribbling in her books. Used to drive Sammy absolutely—"

Masie harrumphed in her chair, slapping her leg with anger. "James, that's enough. Don't speak ill of the dead. I won't have et."

Holly just about fell off her chair in stunned surprise at her blatant hypocrisy. Wasn't it only yesterday Masie had spoken ill of *both* Celeste and Samuel? She ignored her and asked, "James, do you know where her books are?"

James looked at her blankly, empty cup rattling in its saucer, matching time with the tremor in his hand. "Books you say?" He turned to Masie as if to ask for assistance, glanced back at Holly and then sat back in his chair, shaking his head. "I—I don't know." His voice quavered with uncertainty, his brow furrowing with worry.

Scooting to the edge of her chair, ignoring the ramped up glare from Masie, Holly reached over and took the cup from him and placed it on the table. Putting both her hands on his knees, she looked deep into his eyes as she tried to reassure the old man, who'd started to look unsettled and confused. "It's okay, James."

"I, thought, I mean, I'm sorry." James slumped into his chair, shoulders rounding, head dropping down onto his chest. "I forget," he whispered, voice disappearing along with his awareness.

The front door slammed causing the trio to jump in the tense atmosphere. Jack's cheerful voice called from the hallway, "Anybody home?" Two heavy clunks could be heard as he shucked off his work boots.

Masie muttered. "Course we is home. Where else would we be?" She rolled her eyes and crossed her arms across her bosoms in a fit of pique.

Jack walked into the room, unzipping a bright orange pair of work overalls, marred with grease and dirt ingrained into the heavy denim material. His short, dark hair was brown with dirt, and a smudge of dark oil streaked down his face.

Holly felt her face flush. *Even dirty head to toe from work he managed to make her instantly aware of the attraction she felt for him* she thought with exasperation.

Jack's eyes opened wide with surprise, grin spreading ear to ear when he caught sight of Holly. Holly couldn't help herself, she laughed out loud. His eyes were clear, bright, white, stark contrast in his dirty face.

"You're filthy, Jack!"

"You would be too if you were crawling under and over a digger all day! Seemed like I was the only engineer willing to get their overalls dirty today." He shoved the overalls right down, singlet and shorts blindingly clean underneath, muscled arms flexing and bunching as he bent and pulled the legs over his feet and off.

Masie grunted, eyeing Holly as she stared in turn at Jack. "Nice place for a strip tease boy."

Jack laughed, "Sorry Masie. Didn't mean to get you all excited there." He nodded at Holly and smiled at his father. "I'll go have a quick shower and join you all."

\* \* \* \*

Jack joined them half an hour later. Only then did Masie decide to take her leave with a great deal of fussing over James first. She rearranged his blanket over his knee, brushed her hand over his hair, and fluttered around him. He in turn grumbled at the to-do. Holly watched in amusement. It was quite apparent to her that Masie had some sort of crush on the old boy, and he clearly enjoyed it despite the cantankerous show he put on.

She was terribly frustrated as she hadn't been able to discuss her mother's writing with James any further. Masie was distinctly territorial in her attitude toward the old man. He did however seem to rally a little while Jack was in the shower, *maybe knowing his son was home,* she thought. He still seemed a little confused, but entertained Holly with his time as a coxswain in the longboats years before the newfangled "metal contraptions."

"They called us men of steel back then," he said. "Men of steel and boats of wood. It was true too. Only way to get in and out of the harbor was sixteen of us men, eight on each side. No matter if it was sea's as rough as boots, or calm as pond water—if a ship called over the radio that he was going to stop—we went out. Trade to be done you see. The captain would take anything—fish, fruit, curio—any excuse to give the community food or clothing in exchange." James sighed at the memory. "They were good Captains in those days."

"What about now, James" Holly asked grinning. "Would it be men of wood, boats of steel?" Even Masie had laughed and agreed.

Holly was still laughing at his tall tales of big waves and near misses when Jack plopped himself down next to her, smelling of something tangy and citrusy. Her mind stuttered at his closeness and the instant clutch of an invisible hand in her belly.

After Masie had fluttered around James and arranged with Jack to care for his father the next day while Jack worked, she left, not forgetting to glare a goodbye at Holly first. Holly smiled as Masie departed. The atmosphere lightened considerably in her absence.

James smiled benignly at them both and struggled up out of his chair. "I'm tired my boy. I might have a nap before dinner." Jack leapt up to help his dad, and as they shuffled out, James glanced back quickly at Holly with a sly wink and a smile. She grinned at his back as he departed. His ruse to leave them alone was far from clandestine.

While she waited for Jack to return, butterflies swarmed in her tummy. Nerves twanged tighter than a stringed guitar, and threatened to snap as he wandered back in and sat next to her again.

"The old bugger thought we needed time together," Jack said with a twinkle in his eye. "I think he's right." They smiled at each other, grins growing wider until finally they collapsed into laughter.

Jack's laughter died on his lips as he looked into her eyes, and Holly's heart started beating fast in her chest. Searching her face, voice thick with emotion, he said, "I don't think I can keep away from you, or keep things slow Holly."

Her heart threatened the climb into her throat at his words. "I—"

"No, this is right. You know it is. I know it is. It doesn't matter how long we've been together again." He grabbed her hand and turned her body toward him. "This just is."

He leaned in toward her, and claimed her mouth with his She melted into his embrace, knowing somehow, deep down, he was right. It just felt right. Here, in his arms—his mouth on hers—lips teasing hers, tasting, moving tenderly.

They moved jointly, further into the passion of the moment. A moan sighing from her mouth, a groan from him went unheard over the roaring in her head, heart in flight in her chest, and warmth spreading from her belly to the core of her being. His hands were everywhere, in her hair, pulling her to him, and on her back. Obsession deepened the kiss, tongues meeting with desperation.

He nipped at her lip, drizzled kisses along her jawline, and buried his face in her neck. Holly's head dropped back in ecstasy as he inhaled her scent, rained kisses on her heated skin, the hollow of her neck, and across her face to reclaim her swollen mouth.

They broke apart, both breathing heavily, Jack smiling lazily, eyes dark with un-sated lust. "I could do that all day. Who needs a damn job." he said with a grin.

He ran a finger tenderly down her arm, closing his hand finally around hers, squeezing it tight. "So," he drawled slowly. "Are we going to take this how it comes? No pressure no more denials?"

Holly couldn't think of a reason to deny him. This earth shattering, raw emotion surging through her body could not be wrong. She drew in a bone shuddering breath. "No. No more denials."

# Chapter Seven

Holly found the next few weeks becoming routine, a comfort after so many months of upheaval and stress. Once a week she'd visit the store to stock up on necessities, wait till Kristy would finish work, and then she'd risk Kristy driving her home with her groceries. She'd laughingly say payment was coffee for Kristy and a whiskey for her to settle her nerves.

The rest of the time Holly spent writing, visiting James, and then time with Jack. All became a pleasurable monotony—*not,* she thought with a grin. *Jack is anything but boring.*

Rising early every morning she would write, her short story idea blossoming. Her heroine had a richness to her that flowed automatically from her fingers as she typed. She hardly had to think of what the character would say, what she did next. Her heroine's romantic interest just as uninterested as to what Holly had to say or think, he had his own ideas how he wished to progress in Holly's story.

Holly often had to stop, re-read what she'd just written and wonder where it had come from. The plot she'd begun with, no-where near where the characters were pushing her.

She wondered with amazement at how it had developed with such speed, with some revising and editing could be stretched to a small novella. *Using the emotions rich in my life right now,* she thought, *it is no wonder the romantic-themed tale is flowing so well.*

Now, she worried, her life was moving along too well. The constant feeling of waiting for the proverbial shoe to drop, lingered like a black cloud encroaching on a pristine blue sky. The only reason to have such unfounded fears was the unknown—her parents. Every day she had to consciously put those thoughts away, stuff them down, lest they overwhelm her with gloominess.

This Friday afternoon had been blissfully spent with James, Masie nowhere in sight—Sarah taking her turn to sit with James while Jack worked. James, his usual cantankerous self, Sarah doing no right in his eyes compared to the perfect Miss Masie.

James was having a better day today after almost a full week of noticeable deterioration. Holly could see the difference in him just in the short time she spent at the house. She'd been visiting daily, and each change was heartbreaking to see, especially the steep decline in such a short period. Today was special in every way possible. No Masie, and bright and clear-minded James.

As the three of them were enjoying their tea, awaiting Jack's arrival home, James sat back and closed his eyes with a sigh. Holly lifted an eyebrow at Sarah who had settled herself in Masie's usual spot, and nodded in James direction. She'd found that this usually signaled James was ready for a nap, but to her surprise he was far from ready.

"Sarah," he asked, eyes still firmly closed, "I couldn't ask you to make me another cuppa could I?"

Chuffed to be asked for a second cup—usually James grizzled her brew was not strong enough—Sarah bustled off to the kitchen, chest puffed out, full of importance, smiling ear to ear.

Holly gazed at James in amazement. "You just made her day," she said with a laugh. The old man snorted, screwing up his wizened face in amusement. "If I have to suffer through another cup of her watered down piss she calls tea I will, if it means I can get you alone for five minutes!"

Her curiosity piqued, Holly sat forward in her chair, eager to hear what James had to say. Animated, the old man gestured toward the bookcase, packed with books and curio. "You find your mother's books yet, love?"

"No, not yet. There's a room full of boxes and junk at the house, but I've been putting off going through it. I'm hoping they'll be in there."

"Look for a puzzle box. She had to hide her work you see. Sammy didn't like her wasting her time scribbling." He screwed his face up in disgust. "Scribbling. That's what he called it. He had no idea of the talent that woman had. Bah." James crashed his fist down on the arm of the faded and threadbare armchair in frustration.

"She used to steal my books you know. I caught her one day and scared the bejeezus out of her." Laughing fondly, in a haze of memories, he scratched at the white stubble creasing his craggy cheeks.

"I told Celeste that she had to write me an apology. Came back three pages long and was the funniest thing I ever read. That's when I knew she was different—special." He moved uncomfortably in his chair and leaned forward, face sagging with emotion, mouth trembling. Tears welled in his rheumy eyes.

"She had talent, a talent that no one took seriously here, but I *did*. She died for it. It was my fault."

Frozen in her seat, Holly sat with sick, slimy dread slithering up her spine, a lump in her throat making her swallow hard with a dry click. Her father pulled the trigger, not James. What could James have done to promote such murderous rage? Thoughts stumbled over each other trying to digest what James had admitted, trying to understand what he said.

"How could it be your fault James? What did you do?" Anguish twisted Holly's voice, strangled it, sounding so unlike her own, making her wonder, with a brief moment of insanity, who had spoken the words.

James opened and closed his mouth, seeming lost for words. "Find her work, the puzzle box; don't let her work go to waste Holly."

"But, James...what—"

"Here we are, love. Another cuppa as requested." Sarah, blithely unaware of the tension between the two, lumbered happily into the room with her prized cup of tea.

James eyed her offering with distaste. "I don't want that piss water." He batted the cup from her hands, shattering upon contact with the fly-speckled, linoleum floor. "I was talking to Celeste!" He thundered, spittle flying from his mouth, foam gathering in the corners of his wrinkled mouth. Sarah recoiled in horror, wiping spit from her cheek with a shaking hand. She looked from Holly to James with an open mouth, eyes wide with shock.

Face red with anger, James thumped the arms of his chair with his fists. "I. Was. Talking. To. Celeste!" His voice petered out with each declaration, body crumpling back into the chair, as if each spoken word took all the energy he had.

"James!" Holly scrambled from her chair, taken aback by the sudden onslaught. Sarah stood rooted to the spot, shaking violently, mouth opening and closing like a goldfish. Placing an arm on the alarmed woman's arm she turned her body and spoke firmly. "Sarah, clean up the tea, and I'll handle James."

*Oh God, I did this. I caused this.* Holly thought with distress

James rocked in his chair, keening quietly, mouth quivering, eyes blank of emotion. She grabbed both his hands, trying to stop the rocking. Sarah scuttled out to the kitchen, relief oozing from her pores at being given permission to escape. "James, I'm sorry."

James's head lolled back in the chair, eyes struggling to focus on hers. "He's not good enough for you," he whispered weakly, mouth barely moving. "I'm so tired, Celeste, tired of fighting for you. You have to do what I told you. Enough's enough."

Confused and frightened, Holly sunk into a crouch at his feet, laying her head on his knees. What did James tell her mother to do? Why was he fighting? With whom? Sammy?

The keening petered off to a whine. A hand lay warm on her head, stroking her hair back away from her face. Holly looked up at James, his hand falling slack to his side. Tears slid from blank, unseeing eyes. "It's the girl. You have to save the girl."

Holly was horrified at what she'd done to the old man, forcing him to drag up such painful memories, but she was torn. She could risk upsetting him further and dig for answers. He'd brought up more, not solved the ones she already had. She could also do the right thing and settle the old man. Good sense and pure civility told her there was only one choice, one that dictated James health and not her own selfishness.

She knelt in front of him, grasping his hands firmly, looking up into his face. "James, don't worry about Celeste and the girl, stop fighting for now. I'll worry about them myself shall I? We'll look after you right now." She barked a brittle laugh, sounding false even to her own ears.

James seemed not to hear. Closing his eyes, he repeated his words. "So tired."

Sarah hurried back into the room with a bucket, broom, and mop, glancing sidelong at them—young woman kneeling in front of an infirm, old man. Her face was unreadable, blank of emotion or judgment. Sweeping up the broken china, with no nonsense sweeps, she muttered, quietly, "Silly old bugger. I hope I never get like that. Shoot me if I do."

Holly glared, appalled at her insensitivity. Turning back to James she stood and pulled the lever to recline the chair, laying him back. He seemed to already have slipped into a deep sleep, breathing heavy and slow. Pulling the lap rug up higher and tucking it tightly in around him she struggled to push the guilt nibbling at her gut down, tears threatening hot behind her lashes.

*Here I am badgering this man*, she thought, hot with shame. *What kind of person uses a man so ill to find her own answers?* Head down, chin on chest, hair falling loose in a curtain around her face, she leaned over James, hands holding herself up on the armrests of his chair. She felt weak from guilt, and desperation. *James can't be the only one who knows what happened to my mother. There has to be another way to get my answers without browbeating this old man.*

The door slammed signaling Jack's return from work. She jerked in surprise.

Sarah stopped mid sweep, signaling Jack to shush his usual buoyant entry into the house. Leaning on the door jamb he looked from Sarah to Holly standing guiltily beside his father.

Frown puckering his brow, he inspected the shambles with a questioning look at Holly. "What happened?" he asked quietly.

Sarah harrumphed, irritation woven through her voice. "Your dad threw another tizzy is all." She looked darkly at Holly. "Masie warned me not to let her alone with him. He called her Celeste again."

Holly shrugged her shoulders helplessly. She couldn't blame Sarah for being upset with her. James was fine before Sarah left the room, what else could she think. *She was right on the button; I did upset him* she thought, heart heavy with deep remorse.

"We were talking about my mother. He was quite clear and alert, and something slipped." Tears that had been threatening to fall, finally broke through, and left a track of hot wetness down her cheeks. She swiped uselessly at them with the back of her hand. "I'm sorry Jack. I seem to be upsetting people all over the place." She felt utterly miserable. All she seemed to do this afternoon was apologize to people.

Jack hurried to her side, stepping nimbly around the mess in the doorway. Gathering her in his arms he drew her close, shushing her, stroking her back. His sympathy made it one hundred times worse, and she fought to dissolve further into a sob ridden mess. Holly laid her head on Jacks shoulder, giving in to his warm consolation.

James snored gently, moved in his chair, and then broke wind loudly. The sound echoed in the quiet room, Sarah commenting, quietly, "Jesus, James."

Jack's shoulders began to shake under her head, and Holly looked up in surprise. He shrugged, laughing soundlessly. His whole body vibrated against hers. "I can't help it. He always knows how to get the last word, even when he's sleeping."

Holly shook her head as Jack continued his contagious laugh. His eyes twinkled full of mirth. "You're awful, Jack. Poor old bugger."

Jack stepped away and tugged at her to follow. "Come on, we need to talk." Sarah watched them depart, eyeing them with disapproval.

Jack leaned on the railing that encircled the portico. He crossed his arms, staring at her pensively, the humor gone from his face. "Look, Holly. Dad's been up and down all week. You remind him of your mother." Jack looked down at his hands. "You look so much like her, Holly. I don't blame him for mistaking you for her —especially in his condition. These upsets are bound to happen. I understand." He looked up at her. Holly stood before him, nervous to hear the 'but' that was sure to come next.

"Masie's said some things that I'm not sure how to take. Dad's unwittingly made it worse with some things he's said to me. I'm not sure what to think."

Holly grimaced. "I knew that was coming. Do you want me to stay away for a while?"

"No, that's not what I was going to say. Let me finish." He sighed with frustration. "Dad was obviously close to your mum. I'm not sure how...God. I can't even comprehend Dad's involvement..." He paused and looked at her almost pleadingly. "I think I need to know what happened too."

"What did Masie say?"

"It doesn't matter. What she said was pure innuendo, but there's something behind it. There's always a grain of truth in gossip. I just need to find out what that truth is."

"James told me it was his fault."

"What was?"

"I don't know. He wasn't there when my father pulled the trigger...was he?"

Jack reared back like she'd hit him, eyes wide, mouth open in shock. "No!"

"Oh God, I'm sorry Jack. I didn't mean it like it sounded. It's just that he was so upset. He said it was his fault Mum died. I can't see how he'd heap the blame on himself."

"That's what we've got to find out, Holly. I'm in this thing as deep as you are."

Holly sunk down onto the porch step. She hadn't expected this at all. She hung her head as Jack sat beside her. Thigh to thigh, ankle to ankle, he slipped a warm supportive arm around her waist.

In a barely audible whisper Holly said, "Thank you Jack. It means a lot that you're in this with me."

He slid a finger down her jaw line and placed it under her chin. Lifting it , he made her look at him.

"We've always been in it together, Holly." He kissed her gently. "Always."

# *Chapter Eight*

Jack knocked on the door of Holly's house at eight that evening. After Holly left, he'd had a hellish, hour long lecture from Masie, who'd turned up in a hell of a flap. Thanks to Sarah, Masie had been well informed of the afternoon's upset, and had taken it upon herself to give Jack a piece of her mind over his part in it.

"Jack, you know every time ha woman comes to the house, she upsets your father. Why yorley let it continue is beyond me." Masie said, face red with anger.

"Masie, if Dad is upset, there is a reason behind it. He's feeling guilty for something, and Holly reminds him of Celeste. Holly's not here to upset Dad. She likes the old bugger. She's here to visit with him."

"Pah! All the more reason to tell her to stay away. I'm not telling you again, she's trouble, with a capital T. She's not here to *visit*." Masie's mouth had screwed up as she spat out the word. "She's here to find out what her harlot of a mother got up to. She's here to smear Sammy's good name." She pointed a shaking finger at him. "Sammy was my nephew. He was a good man. I won't have her bringing up what he done. It's in the past."

She'd gone stiff with anger, red faced and calm as she'd firmly laid down the law. "If you don't tell ha woman to stay the hell away from James, I will!"

*That's one thing I will not do*, he thought grimly. "She's not being turned away from this house, and that's that, Masie. Deal with it."

Masie scowled at his words. "You es stubborn un. When it all comes down on yous head, don't expect me fer pick up after you." She stuck her hands on her hips and jutted out her jaw, eyeing him with a superior smile. "Since I'm lookin' after yous Dad this night, so you can go off traipsing around with ha floozy of yours, you just pay me mind boy. It will come to a point you *know* I es right, so don't get in over yous head."

It had near killed him to have to bite his tongue, turn his back and walk away. If he had not, both he and his father would have lost out.

He was sick and tired of Masie's interference, and stuck

without her assistance. Masie could do no wrong in his father's eyes and quite frankly was a godsend when it came to his care. She turned up to 'baby-sit' every day, rain or shine, organized care in her place if she was unable to come, and put up with his father's difficult and belligerent ways. She knew she was virtually indispensable and even his worst threat.

The thought of seeing Holly tonight was the only sparkle in the tarnished and contaminated day. The very idea of her made him begin to whistle while he showered, and sing under his breath as he walked in the cool evening breeze to her home.

She welcomed him with a smile, the quick hint of her perfume tickling his senses, caught up in the rush of air as she opened the door. She was dressed in blue jeans so fitting they could have been painted on her slim hips and slender legs. The emerald green halter top she'd added accented those smoky green eyes, and large gold hoops swung from her ears. Her hair usually scraped back in a pony-tail or hanging straight and voluminous, was piled loosely on her head, tendrils escaping to frame her heart shaped face. He stood for a moment and just gazed at her—her ethereal beauty stunning him to silence.

"Close your mouth Jack. You're catching flies." Holly grinned and stepped back so he could enter. "Are you coming in, or are you going to stand out there all evening?"

Bashful at being caught all but leering, he walked in, stopping to kiss her. "You look wonderful. Couldn't help but stare; you're gorgeous." He pulled her into his arms and dropped another kiss on her nose. "We better get going though, or else I'm not going to let you leave the house. This filthy mind of mine has plans of its own."

A pretty pink stained Holly's cheeks indicating her pleasure, *or was it reciprocal desire*, he wondered. She unwound herself from his arms. "I'll grab my coat. I notice it gets cold later in the evenings." The pink stain grew to a rosy red blush as she escaped down the hall. With a giggle underlying the words, she threw over her shoulder. "Your dirty mind can just stew till later."

Her insinuation clear, a rush of blood left his head and traveled straight to his groin. *Down boy*, he thought with a grin. *She could use you as a coat hook if you don't watch out.*

Holly returned, a long woolen jacket half on, in the process of slipping her arm into the other sleeve and flipping the collar back. "Do I need a torch?" she asked.

"Not if we're going the same way after Kristy and Mark's place.

I've got one."

She smiled and stopped in front of him, looking up into his questioning face. He hoped like hell she'd give the answer he wanted.

"No need then."

His dirty mind did a mental high five, while the good side did a little irritating dance of joy. His smile transmitted none of that mental gymnastics, or at least he hoped it didn't. With a little gentlemanly bow he opened the door and ushered her through. "After you."

With a bounce in his step he grabbed her hand, slammed the door closed after them and, they headed off into the moonlit night.

Walking down the driveway and into the dirt road, Jack squeezed her hand. "So. What are we going to do about this Celeste and Sammy thing? Where do we start?"

Holly glanced sidelong at him and squeezed his hand back with a smile. "James told me my mother was a writer. There are supposed to be some books somewhere. I'm assuming they're in a spare room back at the house." She sighed. "It's full of rubbish bags and boxes packed with God-knows what. I'm going to have to go through each one. There's a big stand-alone cupboard in there too, behind stacks of boxes, so that's a possibility."

The breeze picked up, sending the sweet scent of queen of the night flowers into the cool night air. Holly moved a windblown tendril of hair out of her eyes with a backstroke from a finger. *Jesus, even moving her hair from her face is sexy,* he thought.

Mentally slapping his hand with disgust at his one track mind he forced himself to consider what she was saying.

"It's been so long Jack. Would all their personal belongings still be in the house? What if someone's thrown them away?"

"Surely your parents belongings should be stored somewhere, if not in that spare room. It's not logical that they would have been destroyed. Pitcairners are pack-rats, they keep everything for a rainy day."

"I still haven't gotten around to checking what's in there. I don't know if it all belongs to the people that were living in the house before I got there, or to my parents." The frustration in her voice was clear.

He nodded. She had the answer right there. "That's the first step I guess. Go through it." He shrugged. It was a bizarre thing—what did happen to a deceased person's things after they died on Pitcairn? Should it not be held in trust? Properly stored?

"People keep everything here—broken or not. You can't run down to a super-store to pick up a replacement at a moment's notice. My father has things of my mothers, that her mother had passed down to her. Your mum's stuff has to be somewhere, Holly."

When Jack's mother had passed away everything had gone to his father. When Jack's father breathed his last breath, his possessions would be shared amongst his brothers. It was only logical that the same would happen in Holly's case, but if not in the spare room, where would the couple's personal items be?

"I can give you a hand if you like. Two of us going through all the boxes and bags in your spare room will answer the question of who they belong to pretty quick."

There was one other way to confirm what happened to Celeste and Sammy's possessions, which he didn't want to voice just yet— ask his father. His older brothers might also remember better than he. *Idiot*, he rebuked himself, *of course, one of them were bound to know what happened. Why didn't he think of it before?*

"You know, Dad may not be able to shed any light on it, but one of my older brothers may. Mike and Benny were at school in New Zealand, but Brett was here if I remember rightly. He was..." He mentally ticked back the years. "Fifteen when your parents died." Jack slapped his free hand against his thigh. "He was there when you were taken. Do you remember?"

Without waiting for a reply he continued, happy that he might be able to help get some answers without harassing his father. "Brett, Mike, or Benny, they must have talked about it. Any one of them might be able to give us some information."

He smiled at her, his heart lightened, and they continued their walk down the moonlight dappled main road. They lapsed into a comfortable silence, each deep in their own thoughts.

Jack's mood was now buoyant with the thought that he could really help Holly with her quest for knowledge. His recollection of those terrible days focused around her, and the void she'd left when she'd gone.

"I'll ring Brett when I get home from work tomorrow. He might know more than just where their stuff is. He might have overheard more than what he should have—the more serious adult conversations weren't talked about within my earshot anyway."

"Thanks Jack."

Lapsing again in to silence, only the sounds of their feet scuffing in the quiet of the evening, Jack cleared his throat. "Do you ever wonder what it would have been like to have grown up here?"

Holly nodded, smiling sadly. "Yeah, sometimes. Then I think how wonderful my life was with my foster parents, and how much they loved me." She tucked another wisp of unruly locks behind an ear. "I also think about how my real parents died. There must have been a lot of hate between them to depart this life the way they did." Holly bowed her head, watching the ground in front of her as they walked.

"I think if they'd lived, if things had been different, I'd stayed on Pitcairn with parents who obviously hated each other. Would that have changed me for the worse or the better? Would I have been a different person than I am now?"

She looked at Jack, searching his eyes in the darkness. "I had a good childhood Jack, a good life in New Zealand. It may not have been that way here."

"I'm glad. I know your parents used to fight a lot. I heard my parents talking about it once. That can't have been easy for a five year old, but I don't remember you being sad." He sighed. "Maybe I was too young."

"I don't know, or at least I don't remember." She stopped in her tracks, jerking Jack to a sudden stop.

Staring blankly ahead, toward the distant spire of Ships Landing Point looming blackly against the moonlight sky, it seemed to Jack, her eyes were suddenly vacant. A shiver ran through her body and vibrated through his hand, and he watched her in concern as she frowned. "Raised voices maybe," she said slowly, "No. I don't know."

She began walking again shaking her head. "It's best not to dwell on it tonight. I want to have some fun. Argh, I *need* to have some fun!" She dropped Jack's hand and ran ahead, twirling in the road, coat flaring out as she spun like a top. "So much sadness. I've had enough for today. I want to forget, if only for tonight."

She stopped and ran back toward Jack. "One day I'll get my sister Rosy up here. She'll keep you on your toes."

Jack laughed. "I've already got one lady who keeps me at her beck and call. I don't need another." He dropped her hand and slid his arm around her waist as they walked, smiling when she did the same.

He spread his arm out, indicating the island around them. "I think you would have missed this. The complete quiet at night—bar the crickets or the Ghost Birds, no cars or police sirens, loud music blaring or noisy neighbors to break the silence, only nature." He smiled "Apart from my Dad's snoring that is."

"Ghost birds?" Her eyes glinted in the darkness as she smiled.

"They only come out at night, and make a ghostly call. You'll know it when you hear it. No one's ever seen one." He screwed his face into a ghoulish mask, struggling to keep a smile off his lips. "That is alive to tell the tale."

Holly laughed and punched him gently on the arm. "You're a ninny. You're pulling my leg."

"Nope. Well, kinda. There are ghost birds, and they do make that strange night call. We had a scientist camp out up Pawl Valley one night, and he spent half the time searching in vain for one. I suppose there's a real bird name for them, just not on Pitcairn, and no one's seen one."

"Wow. I still don't know if you're just teasing me, but I'll be listening for them now."

Jack smiled. He remembered scaring his brothers one night, hooting right outside the window of their bedroom. Just happened he'd managed to wake up his parents as well, and caught holy hell for being outside alone at night. *Good times.*

Fond memories of the exploits of his childhood brought a warm smile to his lips. *The things he and his friends got up to back then.* He squeezed Holly's waist playfully. "Us kids had the freedom to do anything—playing in the muddy water in the drains at the sides of the roads when the heavy rains came, and swimming in the Bay at the Landing in the hot summer months. God...I used to roam this island when I was a kid, from one end to another. The things I got up to would have made my mother's hair curl."

Nearing the turn off to Marty and Kristy's place he was less than eager to give up his time alone with Holly. Dropping his arm from her waist and grabbing her hand he gave her a sly smile as he tugged, urging her in the opposite direction. "Come on, we'll go sit down at the Edge for a while before we hit the nightlife."

Down at the Edge, they sat overlooking Bounty Bay. Towering above the Landing area, they sat hand in hand on a park bench enjoying the faint sounds of the surf below crashing onto the rocky shoreline.

"Oh God, it's beautiful up here." Holly breathed.

Jack tried to see what she was seeing. He was blind to the beauty of the island now, shades only coming off his eyes when comments were made such as hers.

The towering spire of Ships Landing Point cast black shadows high above them. The peak stood majestic and true, the Bay far below them, water mottled with patches of moonlight, white-caps glowing impossibly bright as the light caught them. The horizon split in two, the inky blackness of the sea, kissing the grey of the moonlight sky. He could smell the salt of the sea, the scent of Lantana bushes scattering the slanted cliff-face before them. Sometimes being blind and suddenly made to see could be an astonishing moment. He sighed heavily at the awe his island inspired when he allowed his eyes to see it.

"If you think this is beautiful, wait till we go on a community trip to Oeno Island. We pack up the longboats and leave the night before, sighting the island first thing in the morning. Now, *that* Island is beautiful. White sandy beaches and the clearest waters you've ever seen."

"Sounds like you're describing a desert island in the middle of nowhere. It's the opposite of Pitcairn, huh?"

Jack laughed. "Yeah, almost. Same isolation, but different in every way. We camp there for two weeks and then come home relaxed and nut brown from the sun. It's the only time us Pitcairners are allowed to truly kick back and do nothing."

Holly nodded. "I've never seen anyone here take a break. Even if they're sitting in a chair, they've got a piece of wood and are busy sanding it, weaving baskets or podding beans. Oeno sounds like a holiday for sure."

Jack turned and ran his hand along Holly's jawline, tucking a finger under her chin, looking deep into her eyes. "You'd love it."

The gentle smile on her face almost undid him. If there was true beauty around him right now, it was her. He shook himself and chuckled with self-conscious laughter. "Well, I suppose we should go kick some butt in a game of darts. What do you think?"

Holly grinned. "I'll probably put more holes in the floor than in the dart board, but why not."

# *Chapter Nine*

Marty's 'Man Cave' was true to its name. Holly followed Jack into a large room pulsing with music, Jennifer Lopez dancing to her latest hit on a big screen, TV hung on a wall above the bar. A large pool table dominated the room. Varnished ply wood walls decorated with pirate flags and large, bleached whale bones hung on prominent display.

Cigarette smoke hung heavily in the air. Music competed with the loud chatter and hoots of laughter coming from the small crowds of people surrounding the bar at one end and dart board at the other. Chairs and couches that had seen their best days long ago, sat along the walls, packed with people relaxing with their drinks, chatting to their neighbors.

It seemed like the whole of Pitcairn had crowded into the large open plan room, but there couldn't have been more than fifteen or sixteen people packed shoulder to shoulder. The atmosphere drew them in with a wave of warmth and hospitality. There were no age barriers here, teens looking as young as seventeen, ruling the pool table, grey haired, chortling and crowing elders at the dart board.

Holly followed Jack through the throng of people, as they wound their way to the bar. A voice screeched excitedly above the fracas. "Holly! Jack! You made it!" Kristy bounced through the crowd toward them, glass of white wine sloshing dangerously close to anointing those she past.

Kristy grabbed Holly by the arm and pulled her away. "Come on, you've got to say hello to Marty." Holly waved goodbye with a smile to Jack, who raised an eyebrow in amusement and waved back. He laughed and called loudly over the noise. "Bring her back with the arm attached Kristy!"

Holly followed the chipper blond. A tall, black haired, and heavily bronzed man, built like the proverbial brick shit-house, stood behind the wood paneled bar, loudly entertaining those standing across from him. Tattoo's radiated from under his singlet and down his arms. Maori tribal designs, undulating around his muscled arms. His audience roared with laughter as he finished his story. Kristy tugged at his shirt.

"Marty, this is Holly."

Marty turned and leaned casually against the bar, eyeing her up and down with appreciation, eyes twinkling with mischief. "Ah...this is why Jack can't seem to concentrate at work lately. Welcome back to the island, Holly."

He grinned at Kristy and clapped his hands together, rubbing them together with glee. "This calls for a welcoming whales tooth don't ya think?"

Kristy rolled her eyes with a fond smile at her partner. "Just the one then." She turned to Holly and gave her a nudge. "This is a tradition here—one Marty takes seriously." She eyed Marty as he grabbed a Tequila bottle and three whales tooth shot glasses, swiping one off him as she spoke. "He takes it too seriously sometimes. It can end up very messy if you don't stop at one."

She brandished one tooth for Holly to see. It looked like what Holly would have expected to see come out of a saber toothed tiger's mouth, not a whale. Curved with a blunt tip, it was hollowed out and had been elaborately carved.

Kristy smiled as Holly traced the outline of the Bounty carved on the side. "Marty's great friends with an American guy who stayed with us once. After a night where Marty drunk him under the table, he vowed to send him smaller glasses, and sent him this. May be the size of a shot glass, but in the wrong hands this little baby can be dangerous!"

Marty chortled as he passed Kristy the rest of the whale's teeth and filled each to the brim with straight Tequila. "It's not the tooth's fault. It's what goes in it. Anyway, Kristy, just having one shot is cheating, love. We'll let Holly off tonight though." He pointed a finger at Holly as he slid the bottle back into its slot under the bar, grinning evilly. "Just tonight."

Kristy passed Holly and Marty a whale's tooth and saluted them both with hers. "To Holly!" With a shy smile appreciating the toast, Holly upended the shot glass and coughed to catch her breath, as the fiery liquid scorched her throat. It left a warm trail as it made its way, burning to her stomach. Grimacing she passed the empty tooth to Marty. "That should keep me warm for a bit, whoooo!"

Marty hooted with laughter. "First one down of many. Wait till you get to play shot glass Battleships."

The thought of a game involving many shots, undoubtedly her being the 'winner', boggled her mind. With a laugh she shook her head. "I think I'll pass. Jack might be up for it though."

"I heard my name, thus I appear." Jack's throaty laugh sounded behind her, his arms snaking around her waist. Holly smiled. "We've just nominated you for Shot Glass Battleships."

He put his chin on her shoulder as he pulled her back toward him, peering over at Marty, eyebrow raised. "No bloody fear mate. You're a dangerous man behind those drinking games. Remember the Shot Glass Olympics?" He shivered, sending vibrations deliciously down Holly's spine. "Nasty stuff afterward, comatose the next day."

Kristy groaned and held her stomach. "Oh hell, yeah, I remember that—half the night, that's a blank—but the next morning was not pretty."

Holly indicated with a thumb toward the whale bones hung on the wall. "Where'd you find those?

Marty peered over her shoulder. "The whale bones? On Henderson, found them washed up on North Beach, bleached clean in the sand. Must have been there a while. Fell over them actually." He winked at Kristy. "That's what we tell people anyway."

Kristy swatted him good-naturedly. "I was watching him fishing off the reef, kicking my feet in the sand, and there they were. We get Humpbacks passing the island August/September, so it must have been from one of those pods."

She collected the empty shot glasses and placed them upside down on the bar.

"Anyway I'm stealing Holly; we're going to take our drinks down the other end of the house." Kristy topped up her own glass, and poured Holly a chilled chardonnay. "Come on Chook."

Holly left Jacks embrace with a tinge of regret, and followed Kristy down a hallway to a comfortable lounge. The music and the noise from the Man Cave muted to a dull roar.

Curling her legs under her as she sat in an overstuffed armchair, Holly took a sip of the cold, crisp wine, letting it wash away the aftertaste of Tequila. Kristy folded herself into a chair opposite and toasted her with a grin. "I'm glad you made it. We'll go join them later for a game of darts, but first I wanted to let you know, I've been doing some digging for you."

"You did? About Mum and Dad?"

"Yeah, but don't get excited, because what I've found out ain't good." Kristy's face twisted into a frown of aversion.

Holly rolled her eyes. *Nothing's ever good news with my parents.* "Don't worry, you probably know more than I do. Anything is better than nothing."

"Disclaimer though, before I start. You know that the island loves to gossip, and what I've heard may be just that. So take it with a grain of salt Okay?"

Holly nodded and leaned forward, listening with anticipation. *This is like a puzzle. Getting pieces one by one, each not yet fitting to the other. One day, I'll have the whole set, and a picture would emerge, I can understand.*

"The rumor is that Sammy liked to use his fists He and your mother did more than argue. It got physical. No one ever saw bruises, but people knew what was going on. They're saying something was going on between James and Celeste, and that's why Sammy was pushed over the edge."

Kristy slammed her glass down on a small table next to her chair, wine slopping over the edge, face screwed up with irritation. She licked the wine that had splashed onto her fingers off and continued, voice shaking. "The thing that *really* pisses me off? The way these bastards talk about Sammy like he could do no wrong—like he was right to hit her." She shook her head angrily. "Doesn't matter what you do, a man hitting a woman is wrong, full stop!"

Holly took a large swig of wine from her glass and leaned back against the chair, dropping her head back to stare unseeingly at the ceiling.

"Kristy, it just gets worse and worse." *James had declared it was his fault Celeste died. Why? The rumors about Mum and Dad, and why he killed her. Could it get any worse?*

"You've got to remember it is all just gossip love."

"No, no, it isn't." Sitting back up, she fixed her eyes on Kristy's with a steeled look of pain. "I remember the arguments. Loud voices. Jack and I were talking about this earlier and a memory came back that shook the living bejeezus out of me."

Tears welled at the corners of her eyes and she swiped them angrily away with the back of her hand. "I couldn't tell him. He was talking about calling one of his brothers, asking him for help about something else. He was just so pleased with himself. I didn't want to take the wind out of his sails with another crappy thing I'd remembered."

Kristy smiled sadly and came and sat next to Holly, perching on the arm of the chair and pulling her into a one-armed hug. "I think he would have understood Holly. What did you remember?"

"It was dark and I was sitting in my bed, this stupid floppy eared bunny in my arms." Holly snorted a hiccupping laugh, wiping more tears that rolled defiantly down her cheeks. "I remember a damn bunny better than my own parents."

"I could hear my mother crying—my father shouting. That noise of skin hitting skin, slaps and punches. I remember knowing I had to stay silent so they didn't know I could hear. How's that for a charming childhood remembrance? A five year old knowing she couldn't protect her mother from getting hit?"

"Geez." Holly gratefully accepted a handful of tissues from Kristy and scrubbed at her face, hoops in her ears jiggling madly against the side of her face. "Sorry, Kristy. Just what you needed, a bawling woman dumped in your lap."

Kristy laughed lightly and patted Holly's shoulder. "S'all right, no one dumped on anybody. It's what friends are for right?"

Eyeing Holly with a shrewd look, Kristy retreated back to her chair. "I have one more piece of advice though. I worked in the Island Secretary's office for a while and there is a safe with all the wills in it. I'm sure there is one envelope there with your parent's names on it. You need to check that out."

"I didn't find a will in the box of information I found at my foster parents. I didn't think there was one." Holly stared with excitement at Kristy. "I'll check that out."

"Ask for Cheryl. She's the secretary at the moment, she'll help. In fact, I'll come with you if you want a little bit of support, but she's great. She'll look after you, I promise."

Kristy leaned back in her chair and gave Holly a speculative look. "We'll finish our drinks and head down to join the boys. First you need to fill me in on what's going on between you and Jack!"

Holly laughed at the obvious ploy to change the subject. "He's wonderful. I just feel like—this is so corny—I never thought I'd hear it coming out of my own mouth—he's my soul mate." She waited for the howl of derision from Kristy with this comment, but Kristy nodded sagely.

"It's *so* not corny." She swatted the air with her hand. "Well I would have thought so before I met Marty, but not now." Kristy leaned forward in her chair. "So...you love him?"

Holly blanched and then blushed furiously. "Oh God, I don't know, that's a big word with big emotions behind it. It's only been—what—three weeks? I know I think about him all the time. I'm a dribbly mess on the floor when he kisses me, and I 'lust' him, but love? I don't know."

*If my past relationships are anything to go by, what do I know about love anyway*, she thought. *No man in my life before had made me feel as safe or...*she grinned at the thought. *Make* *me burst into passionate flames inside with burning desire, at only a touch from his hand, or a kiss from his lips.*

She looked at Kristy, eyes twinkling. "I wouldn't carve our names into a tree and surround it with a love heart yet, but he light's my fire, if you know what I mean."

Kristy roared with laughter and clapped her hands in approval. "Marty would be an arsonist if we went down that track. He lights my proverbial fire every chance he gets!"

It seemed to Holly that time flew past too fast. A bottle of wine disappeared and a second one opened, when Jack sauntered down the hall to find them. She was in fits of giggles, tears of laughter streaming from her eyes. Kristy was waving her arms with gusto as she regaled her with a Henderson Island exploit.

"Wondered where you two had gotten to! What's so funny?"

Kristy winked at Holly and grinned at Jack, hooking a thumb back in the Man Cave's direction. "Your mate out there actually. Was just telling Holly about that time it was his turn to clean out the camp toilets."

"Oh Jesus. The time he fell in, or the time it broke down on him?"

Holly broke into a fresh set of giggles, her breath coming in pants and gasps as she struggled to speak between uncontrollable fits of laughter. "He fell *in*?"

"Yup, I've never seen a man so tanned turn so green. Kermit the frog would have been jealous."

Jack snickered. "Kristy can fill you in on that revolting story back at the Man Cave. Half the crowd's left already and we need another pair for the dart tournament—you two are up!"

# *Chapter Ten*

Holly and Jack stumbled, buzzing with happiness out of the Man Cave, waving cheerful good-byes to Marty and Kristy. It was an ungodly hour of the morning and Holly was just starting to feel the effects of a third attempt at a whale's tooth shot. The cool air hit her with a slap, sobering her a little, head throbbing in the quiet as they strolled away from the pounding music and smoky air of Marty's party den.

As Holly tripped inelegantly over a non-existent obstacle she giggled, glad for Jacks supporting hand. "Oops, I think that last shot took me past tiddly to slightly sloshed."

"Tiddly or not, I still can't believe you beat us in that last game. Shocked the hell out of Marty."

Holly giggled. "Shocked me too." She glanced at Jack, his face glowing serene in the moonlight, a smile playing around his lips. "I had fun tonight. Thanks Jack, it was just what I needed."

"It was good to see you laugh."

"It was nice to be amongst friends. To feel normal again."

They silently walked back the way they'd came just a few hours before, hands clasped tightly. Their pace was slow, the hum between them thrumming with unconscious want.

Just before they reached the turn to his house, Jack squeezed her hand, and brought her to a stop, drawing her close into his arms. "We have to make a choice now." He searched her face, staring deep into her eyes.

Holly's heart hammered and rose into her throat as he caressed her cheek, cupped her chin and kissed her with tender slow resolve. Slipping his arms around her, hands nestling into the curve of her lower back, he pulled her against him.

She felt her face heat and flush with his touch. She became aware of his growing excitement pressing hard against her. She shivered with a desire, her body growing liquid in response to his clear signal of longing.

Jack pulled away, his face shadowed with moonlight and lust. "Do we go straight on to your place? Do I drop you home alone? He paused. "I want you to come home with me, Holly. Masie is there tonight for Dad, but I still don't want him to wake in the morning without me. I need you with me. You make me feel like I've loved no one else. You're the one. You've always been the one."

Holly's breath caught in her throat, emotion thickening her voice. "Yes, Jack. I'm not fighting this anymore. Take me home with you."

He kissed her, mouth tender, cementing the knowledge deep in her heart that she'd made the correct choice. It felt so right, this next step they were going to take.

The short walk to Jack's house was over in an instant, though Holly had no idea how she' got there. Her feet was an inch off the ground, as she floated on Jack's arm. Where twenty minutes before she'd felt fuzzy from the alcohol, now it was with anticipation. Every accidental touch sent shock waves in her belly.

The last two steps to his porch seemed like Mount Everest. At the summit, Jack turned to her on the darkened porch. In shadows, hazy with emotion, without words, their worlds collided. They melted into each other's arms, primal need driving them far beyond normal control and civility.

Mouths hot, gasping, moans of passion the only communication needed.

\* \* \* \*

Jack moved her back, sudden desperate need for her multiplied as she groaned her assent. He pushed her up against the closed door, whispering hot kisses over her face, tasting her excitement. His hands at her waist, he slipped them under her halter top and ran them up her slender frame. Groaning into the hollow of her throat, his hands touched the silk of her bra and the warm firmness of her breasts.

She closed her eyes tight with the agony of the hunger for his touch. She gasped as his thumbs made slow swirls around her nipples, erect with desire. Waves of pleasure radiated out from his combined ministrations to her breasts and his mouth as it traveled back up her slender neck to her mouth. He claimed it, kissing her hard, passion overcoming good sense.

With a guttural moan he lost control as her mouth responded to his urgency. Lifting a taut, denim clad thigh, she curled her leg around his waist, tilting her hips, and opening herself up to him. His mind tipped into madness as he realized if they were naked, he could plunge into her right now, deep into the very core of her.

He pulled away from her and she whimpered at the loss. Breath jagged, voice harsh with wanting, he spoke, "I'm not waiting another minute. I have to have you."

Holly laughed a shivery, brittle laugh. "You could have had me right out here." She'd been lost in the moment, the passion overwhelming her to the point of thoughtlessness.

He pulled her to him, kissed her once more and stepped around her to open the door—and stepped into hell.

Lights blazed, blinding him after the darkened porch. Masie stood arms crossed, face creased into a scowl of distaste in the middle of the hall. Hair in curlers, and dressed in a baggy, stained nightgown, she looked like a caricature of the frumpy housewife. All she needed was the rolling pin tapping in her hand and she'd be frightening. In his current state, she was the last person he wanted to see. He froze at the look in her eyes, not only distaste, but pity lay in those depths.

Holly stepped into the hall behind him, a husky laugh in her voice. "What are you waiting for? I thought—" Her voice faded as she understood.

"Masie."

The old woman's face twisted into a vestige of disdain as she looked down her nose at Holly. "I should have known it was you out there with this poor deluded boy."

Masie turned to Jack, with a growl of disgust. "You could have woken your father with the filthy noises you were making out there with that...that—hussy." The last word came out with a hiss, and a glare of revulsion, lips pulling back from her mouth in a scowl of contempt.

Jack recoiled in anger. "Masie, you have no right—"

"I. Have. Every. Right." Masie spat, voice shaking with pure rage. She pointed a trembling hand at Holly, yet she directed her venom at Jack. "That girl yorley so keen to ride, could very well be yous own sister. I warned you Jack. I tell yorley that yous father done wrong. I *warned* you."

Holly turned to Jack, eyes wide with horror, mouth crumpling in shock. "You knew I could be your sister? But...What we were doing out there..." She backed away from him, until the wall prevented her from going farther. She looked like she wanted to be anywhere but here, away from Masie, the accusations, from him. He cowered inwardly at her slack-jawed shock, her face pale, her eyes wide with disbelief.

Jack shook his head against Masie's shocking statements. He would not believe his father capable of such a thing. He loved his mother. He'd seen the way they loved each other. There was no way.

He stared at Holly. She stood frozen against the wall, visibly shaking, eyes welling with tears. With shock, he realized there was anger in those eyes. He implored forgiveness, putting his palms out in contrition and stepped toward her, but she cowered from his touch. He felt sick at her rejection, sick at the accusations.

He turned back to Masie, who stood arms crossed, gleam of satisfaction in her eyes, a thin smile on her lips. "Es about time yorley realized. I can see et in yous face, Jack. I'm pleased you es finally know the truth."

*She was happy at the heartache she'd caused.*

"Nothere's no way Masie." He shook his head firmly rejecting her revolting suggestion. "You es one sick old woman. Yorley es wrong." He slipped into the speech of Pitkern as his mind whirled with pain. "Look at us. Holly es blond and green eyed. I gut brown eyes, brown hair. We es nothing alike."

Masie's arms tightened with indignation across her breasts. "Of course you es nothing alike. She take after her whore of a mother. You take after your father. Her mother was jest the same as her. She es one apple dropped not far from ha tree." She spat in Holly's direction. "You es ought to be feeling ashamed. You es just like her, ready to open yous legs to any hard cock that flaps in yous face." Masie shook her head. "I'm not going to stand by this time and watch. I did it once before when James was fooled by Celeste, watched her wind him around her little finger, treating her husband like a cuckolded fool. I won't let her daughter destroy you too, Jack."

"What you're doing now Masie—*that's* destroying me—*you're* destroying me."

He ran his hand through his hair, hands shaking. "None of this can possibly be true. I don't believe it of my father. It's just convenient he can't defend himself, the way he is now."

Masie's mouth twisted, her lips curling back in disdain. "You carry on like you are without finding out the truth, you es as sick as ha gal fer yorley."

Holly let out a choked, strangled cry and ran from the house, Jack helpless to stop her, and not blaming her for wanting to escape the madness.

Jack steeled himself against the murderous rage that now burned deep within his gut. His first instinct was to throw Masie out on the street behind the escaping Holly and tell her to apologize to her for the filth that had spewed from her mouth. Hell, he wanted to tell her never to darken his door again. His broken heart told him he couldn't even do that. His own father relied on this monster in an old woman's body, too much.

"Go home Masie." He sighed. "Go home. Realize this though. If no other threat has stuck in that dirty little mind of yours, let this one stick now." He stared at Masie, eyes flashing, mouth set in a firm line. He spoke quietly, but in a tone that let her know in no uncertain terms what he was about to say was meant seriously. "If you ever, ever speak ill of Holly's mother, Holly, or my father again, you will never set foot in this house again."

\* \* \* \*

Holly ran from the house, belly rebelling, nausea rising as the nightmarish words echoed in her mind. The horror of Masie's accusations were screaming in her head, battling for attention. *Jack could be my brother. He could have been my lover. He knew it was a possibility and still he said nothing, still touched me like a lover, held me close, said loving words to me.* She stumbled headlong from the house, tripped mindlessly down the steps, and fell hard to the ground on her hands and knees.

Stomach heaving with too much alcohol and the shock of revelation, Holly vomited. Arms and legs like jelly, she struggled to keep upright as she vomited again. She wished she could expel the memory of the last horrifying moments as well.

Belly heaving, breath coming in gasps, voices loud and accusing behind her, she scrambled to her feet and ran into the darkness.

\* \* \* \*

Jack found her sitting in the darkness, waiting for him on her front porch steps.

"I knew you'd come." Her voice flat, devoid of feeling.

He stood before her, unsure what to do, his world upside down and back to front.

"Of course I'd freaking come. I couldn't leave it like that."

Her face in shadows, she sat head bowed, hands clasped around her bended knees. "Why didn't you say something, Jack?"

"Because it's not true Holly—Dad wouldn't, couldn't —"

"How would you know?" Her voice raised to a screech. Holly

stood and moved toward him, fists clenched. "You were too young. You said so yourself, tonight. You didn't know what the adults where doing. But, you knew there might be a possibility we may be half brother and sister!" She sobbed, her face twisted with pain, and she dropped her head into her hands. "You let it go too far, you should have told me."

Jack put his hands on her shoulders to comfort her, but she moved back from him with a jerk.

"No!"

"Holly, *please* forgive me. This is tearing me up inside too. I'm in love with you, *please*."

She shook her head, tears on her cheeks glistening in the moonlight. "No, Jack," She whispered his name. "I can forgive you, but you can't touch me. You can't say those words to me. If Masie's right..." She sobbed, voice breaking with emotion. "If it's true, it's sick, Jack."

"Holly, I know in my heart this is not true. Don't cut me off, don't push me away." Jack felt his heart tearing in two, the tears on her face, the pain in her voice, trebling the heartache.

"Just go, Jack. Please. I'm begging you. We can't do anything more tonight except hurt each other more." She stood, and backed away from him, chest heaving with sobs, loud in the quiet of early morning.

He swiped angrily at his own tears that fell unbidden and rolled coldly down his cheeks. "Okay, I'm going, but I won't stop telling you I love you. That's the one thing I know is true. I'll be back. I'll keep coming back until we find out the truth."

Holly turned her back on him and walked up the porch steps, opening the door to the house. She paused, head down, hand on the knob, voice trembling with emotion. " If you can't do as I asked, don't come back at all."

Holly stepped into the darkness of the house and closed the door with a gentle click.

Jack let the pain overtake him and moaned silently to the night's sky.

# *Chapter Eleven*

He felt like he had sand in his eyes. He sat on the side of the bed and yawned, stretched and then rubbed at his face. He felt like absolute crap. Glancing at his watch and finding it was only eight o'clock, he could understand why he was absolutely buggered. *Four hours sleep. If you could call it sleep.* Dreams had plagued him, nightmares of falling, running through banyan tree filled valleys that never seemed to end and Holly. Her face, streaked with tears, pushing him away. He moaned and ran his hands through his hair.

Pulling the covers into a messy semblance of a made bed, he stumbled to the bathroom and splashed cold water on his face. Staring into the mirror, face dripping, he scratched absentmindedly at the five o'clock shadow on his cheeks. *Right, buck up or shut up. This rubbish has to end right now. Call Brett today—this morning.* Mind settled now he had a plan of action Jack shaved quickly, dressed and was making coffee when he heard his father shuffling down the hall.

"Morning, Dad. Want a cuppa?

"Yes, thanks, boy. Where's Masie?"

Jack was glad he had his back to his father as he fished around for an extra mug and tea bag in the cupboards. His face screwed into a scowl at the mere mention of her name. "I'd say she'll be up late this morning. She'll probably be in the spare room still sleeping."

"Harrumph, not like her to be a slug-a-bed. She usually has my porridge ready by now."

Jack sighed. She was the last person he wanted to see this morning, her snores as he'd walked past the spare room a welcome noise. He had no plans to work today. She wouldn't be here long. Saturday's were his day with his Dad. "I'll make it for you this morning. Let her have the day off, Dad. Saturday, remember?"

His father grunted. "You don't make it right."

"Jesus, Dad." Jack poured the hot water into the cups and plopped his father's hot drink in front of him. He'd taken his usual seat at the table and was wearing a petulant frown, his eyebrows drawn together like two furry caterpillars meeting for a kiss.

"Porridge is porridge. How can anyone get that wrong?"

"Well, you manage to. If yous father not happy that es." Masie stood in the kitchen doorway, dressing gown pulled tight around her pudgy middle. A self-satisfied smile creasing her lips. She bustled in, pulling a pot out of the cupboard under the sink and started searching for the porridge.

"Leave it Masie. I'll do it. You can go home, get ready for church." *In other words, hurry up and bugger off, you petulant woman. The sooner I see the back of you the better.*

Masie stood at the kitchen bench, measuring out porridge into the pot. "Yorley can't stand me for half an hour more? Yous must have got out of the wrong side of bed dis morning."

Jack could hear the smile in her voice, and he felt the burn of anger start to bite in his belly. "I'm perfectly capable of making my own father's breakfast on my only day off. To be perfectly honest, I wouldn't mind seeing the back of you this morning."

Masie slammed the pot on the oven top and clicked the gas lighter to start the flame. She whirled to face him, dressing gown sleeve dangerously close to catching the blue flame now dancing under the pot. "Why? Yorley upset I been tell yorley two the truth? You should be glad I had the guts for tell ha woman. Yous nor mean to tell her at all. Shame on you boy."

Jack shook with anger, fists clenching. "Why, you —"

"Oh, for God's sake. Yorley two stop yous arguing in there. Sounds like two cats fighting over a rat." James roared from the dining room. "I just want my breakfast, not World War three!" He began coughing, a harsh, rattling bark. Jack hurried in to pat and rub his back. Mornings were hard for James. His chest seemed to fill with phlegm overnight, and cause him great distress when he arose. He hacked and spat into a handkerchief, inspected the contents, then rolled it into a ball and shoved it back into his pants pocket. Jack grimaced. *Yuck, must remember that when I put the next load of wash in.*

"Did you take your pills?" Masie called from the kitchen.

"No, woman. I've only just got up meself. Jacks just got me cuppa tea."

Masie waddled in with his tablet tray, an assortment of different colored and sized capsules sorted into days. She flicked Saturday's allotment into James shaking hand as Jack watched. *One for his heart, one for gout, one to thin his blood...Geez there must be at least eight or nine there for him to take.*

"I don't know why you don't rattle when you walk, Dad."

"Called old age son. You'll get there too one day." He used his cup of tea to wash the pills down one by one, passing Jack his now empty cup. "Now if yorley two aren't going to fight over it, you can refill ha cup. Please."

Jack smiled. Dad won't admit it, even under torture, but he enjoys the fuss. He refilled the cup and brought it to the table as Masie served James his breakfast. She glared at Jack. "If yorley don't mind, I'll have some myself and then I'll go. If I have permission that is."

Jack rolled his eyes and shook his head. "When have you ever asked my permission?"

James grunted and glared at the two of them over a steaming spoon of porridge. "Children!"

Jack couldn't help it. He laughed out loud. Mornings were his favorite time with his dad. The time where he seemed the most like his old self. If you disregarded the struggle of old age problems, his dependence on his pills, and the many wrinkles on his sweet face, he almost seemed like the man he knew so many years ago. *It's what breaks my heart the most. Dad being Dad in the mornings, then coming home at night and seeing the confused, sick man he's become.* He dropped his head to sip his coffee, lest his father see the sadness in his eyes. *Damn the Alzheimer's to hell.*

The morning seemed to drag. He did the chores that built up during the week, the laundry, cleaning the bathroom, changing sheets on both his and his fathers bed. It took his mind off Holly, and the knowledge he had to wait till he could call his brother. In New Zealand they were a day ahead and three hours behind Pitcairn time, so he couldn't call until at least eleven am, where it would be eight in the morning Sunday there.

When it finally rolled achingly slow to eleven, he checked on his father and then took the cordless phone outside onto the porch.

"Mmm, Hello?"

"Brett, Wut-away."

"Jack? You know what time et es?" A mighty yawn echoed down the phone line.

"Yeah, sorry, Brett."

"On a blinking Sunday morning too. You do know we treasure our weekends here, Bro!"

Jack cringed. Brett worked as an engineer for a shipping company at the Auckland City wharf, and long hours were the norm. "I know, Brett, sorry. I just have some issues up here, and need your help."

Jack could hear Brett's wife in the background asking sleepily who was on the phone. "Go back to sleep, love. Jack's on the phone." To Jack he said, "Hang on little brother. I'll just get up and let Michelle go back to sleep."

After a few minutes of muffled noises, bangs and the sound of running water, Brett came back on the line. "I'm gonna need a coffee for this ain't I?"

"Yup. Big trouble in little China here."

"Oh, Jesus, what's wrong with Dad?"

Jack laughed. "No, it's not Dad, he's fine. Well, normal anyway. He's getting worse, but it's expected. No, it's Holly."

"Holly...Holly...Oh, Holly Christian? When did she get back to the island?"

"A month ago now, hell, it's gone by so fast." Jack scratched his head, *had it really only been four weeks since she'd come back?*

"So, what's up? You two thick as thieves again, I bet."

Jack's mouth turned up at the corners, then, the smile faded. "Yeah, you could say that. Brett, Masie's been stirring up some trouble about Dad and Celeste. Do you remember much about them?"

Brett swore. "Nasty piece of work. She hasn't changed much, old Masie." The phone crackled as Brett moved about. "Dad and Celeste...She was over at our house all the time. Used to piss me off a bit, actually. I'd come home from school and there she'd be with Dad at the kitchen table with her books. Dad would be leaning over her, checking her spelling, or God knows what. Why?"

"Masie says that Dad and Celeste were having an affair."

A bark of laughter hummed over the phone line. "Dad? No freaking way. Mum would have killed him. He would've been without his nuts if he'd gone anywhere near another woman. God, those rumors are so old they should be moldy by now."

"Yeah, that's what I thought too. Mum would have killed him. Masie's stirring up a hornets nest here, with rumors about what Dad and Celeste were up to. I just had to ask." Jack sighed. "Holly and I went out last night to Mark's and came back home and Masie was up waiting for us. Told Holly we could be half brother and sister."

Brett let fly a barrage of swear words that would make a sailor blush. "Of course, she's Dad's big, bad body guard now. I can't believe the cr...hang on a minute, you were bringing Holly home? Whooo, you dirty little bugger! Little brother, you work fast!"

Jack grinned a humorless grin. "Didn't work out the way we'd planned. We got an earful instead. Holly left in tears, and understandably so. She's special, Brett. It's not just...I don't know. It's not just fun, me and Holly I mean." He sighed. "I love her." Saying it baldly like that to his big brother after the hurt and pain of the early hours of this morning, felt like another arrow to his heart.

"Let me think, Jack. It's too early in the morning." Brett puffed out air into the mouth piece, making Jack pull the phone away from his ear for a second with a wince.

"Okay, work it back. Holly's two years younger than you, right?"

"Yeah."

Brett's voice got faint as he worked back. "You were born in... so..." Brett paused for so long that Jack almost asked if he was still on the line. "Holly would have...Jack, I think Dad was in New Zealand for medical around the time Celeste and Sammy went to New Zealand to have Holly. Celeste would have had to been about six months pregnant—that's when they usually send mother's out. Dad had gone for major surgery—remember? He'd had heart bypass. He was there for over a year. Oh, God, yes. Mum and Dad had already been in New Zealand when Mum was pregnant with you—went back to Pitcairn, and then Dad had to turn around and go straight back out for his heart. It was a tough time for us, with Mum and a baby, plus us four rabble rouser's."

Jack's knees went weak as Brett spoke. Did the time frame work? Could Dad just be a victim of vicious lies? *Oh, please let the timing work out.*

"How can I make sure of dates though? This is really important."

"Sounds it little brother. You sound really cut up about this."

"I am. She is. It about broke my heart to see her last night. She...she told me we couldn't see each other till we knew what the truth really is."

Brett sucked in his breath. "Check Dad's old passports. Does he still keep everything in that box under the bed? If they're there, they'd be in that box."

"I'll check."

"Jack?"

"Yeah?"

"Let Masie's rubbish go. She had a thing for Dad years before Mum and Dad got together. She hated Mum. She used to say and do things that would have Mum in tears. She hated Celeste too. I was old enough to be aware of the trouble she was causing, wasn't deaf to the rumors that she was spewing. She's a poisonous woman. She's in her element right now helping you look after Dad. If I was you, I'd tell her to sod off, it's not worth the energy or the trouble."

"I can't. It's not me—it's Dad. He's come to depend on her, and I have to work. She goes, and I have to stop work, which means we don't eat, or she stays, and I'm up nights worrying what else is going to fall out of the old bag's mouth."

Brett sighed. "Sorry, Bro. Sometimes I think us kids left you with the brunt of it with Dad. There's just nothing for us at home anymore. No work, no money. Michelle wants to come home, bring the kids back to see the island one day. Right now though, we just can't afford it."

Jack shook his head. "No, I understand, Brett. Give those two boys of yours a hug from their Uncle Jack for me."

"I will. Hang on." Jack could hear Michelle's voice buzzing in the background, Brett explaining why he'd called. The phone crackled and hummed as it was passed over and Michelle's voice came on the line.

"Hey, Jackie-boy. If there's a wedding, we're coming home. Bugger the expense." The smile in her voice was infectious and Jack laughed out loud.

"If there's a wedding, then there's been a miracle, and I'm converting immediately."

Michelle sniffed. "Don't let that woman get your knickers in a twist. She's a miserable old sod, who's only happy when everyone else is wallowing in the mischief she's created. Brett's right. Kick her to the curb."

"I love you, Michelle. You always know just the right thing to say."

"Ha. One Quintal male's quite enough to handle, thank you." Michelle paused. "Love you too, Jackie-boy. Look after yourself, okay?"

Jack hung up the phone feeling one hundred times better. *Now, if only he could find the proof behind Brett's thinking, he'd be golden.*

# *Chapter Twelve*

Holly awoke with a start, pillow damp under her cheek. The bright sun heated the room. The sheets twisted around her body in a nasty snarl, damp from the sweat that seemed to run in rivulets from her naked body. She rolled over, hair stuck to her forehead and cheeks. She ran her hand through her knotted hair, and checked her watch, shocked to see it was after midday.

For a few moments she was disorientated, blank, head fuzzy with sleep and her eyes puffy from…She remembered, and her world came crashing down around her ears again.

She'd closed the door on Jack's heartbroken face early that morning, heart shattering into a trillion pieces. Sliding down against the door, she sat on the cold, hard floor and let her own tears and pain loose, crumpling in a boneless mess on the floor. She'd lain there until she was sure a puddle had formed from her tears, and there were no more left to fall. Dragging herself down the hall, she collapsed into her bed and stared into the dark, eyes dry, mind void. She thought she'd never sleep. She hoped when she did, she'd never wake. Her life felt so broken. Holly had no idea where to turn next.

Sleep did come—finally—though it was not an escape. It was filled with dreams, restless snapshots of Jack, raised voices—and hell.

Holly untangled herself from the bed and sat on the side, head hanging. She pulled her hair back out of her face, and sat upright. Taking a deep breath, she stood, dragging the covers, sheets, and pillow cases off the bed, dumping them in the hall. "I'm not going to be that woman," she muttered. *I'm not going to let Masie, or James, my parents, or Jack for that matter, turn me into a sniveling mess.*

Standing under a lukewarm shower, Holly shivered as she washed her hair, scrubbed her body clean. *If only I scrub my mind clear of last night's memory*, she thought wryly. *If only it were that easy.* The normality of drying off, dressing, brushing her hair, and dumping the bedding in the laundry settled her rattled nerves a little. A void still seemed to yaw in her mind. She tried to stamp it down with conscious ferociousness, but she could not forget his heartbroken wail as she turned her back on him. She had no other choice. The thought opened a new wound in her heart. She put her hand to her chest against the pain.

In the kitchen she put on coffee and stood leaned against the kitchen bench, looking blindly out the window. Writing just didn't seem like something she could face right now She'd probably end up killing one or the other of her main characters in spite. She laughed bitterly.

As the kettle boiled and clicked off, she poured a steaming, strong cup of coffee, added sugar, and milk, and moved down the hall to the spare room. Standing for a moment in front of the closed door, she finally leaned forward, without taking a step. She turned the handle and pushed the door, letting it swing open with a bang as it collided with the wall inside.

Stuffy, still overcrowded with boxes, bags, and covered with a layer of dust, it seemed claustrophobic and far too small. Holly took one step back, almost turned on her heels to leave, and then shook herself with disgust. Smiling nervously at her own reaction, she wondered what she'd expected to find. Maybe that the same fairy who'd left the bread and fruit when she'd arrived would have been busy in here too? Kindly left a neat pile labeled 'Celeste's Stuff', a neon sign pointing to a pile of books with her mother's name on it?

Steeling herself, she took a few steps into the room, setting her coffee down on a sturdy looking box and dragging a dusty, black plastic bag, soft and pliant with it's contents. Untying the bag she found sheets, towels, and face cloths. The rest of the plastic bags held much the same. She stood for a moment and stared at the bag in her hands. On a sudden impulse, she hefted and threw the bag with all her might into the hall, towels and linen spilling out in all directions as it hit the wall and imploded. She screamed with rage, loss and frustration, hitting the bags with her fists, spilling more linen on to the floor as she vented her anger at Jack, and at herself.

Finally spent, she lay on the floor in the midst of the pile of laundry, hysterical bubbles of laughter boiling from the depths of her belly. Holly laughed until her stomach hurt and the laughter became tears. Pressing her face into her hands she vowed this would be the last time she cried for something she couldn't change.

By late afternoon, Holly sat dirty, hot, and tired in the middle of the spare room, belly grumbling. She'd gone through the mess, and restored the room to some semblance of order.

She had no idea if they bags belonged to her parents, or the last tenants. She put them to one side of the room. The boxes, which she'd only just begun to tackle, were now stacked neatly on the other side of the room next to the large cupboard.

First though she realized, she'd have to eat. She was starving, she hadn't eaten breakfast. Even the coffee she'd made earlier still sat untouched and cold. The rumble of a bike outside indicated her belly would have to wait a little longer.

Peering warily out the window she heaved a sigh of relief as she realized her visitor was Kristy, not Jack. She didn't know what she would have done if it had been the latter. *Hide?*

She smiled. As if she could on this island. Everyone already knew everybody else's business. Half the island probably knew about the fight with Masie and Jack last night. The other half was probably making something up more juicy. *What could be more juicy than possible incest?* The thought made Holly feel icy cold. She suppressed an involuntary gag. Her hunger disappeared. Her tummy roiled with distaste.

Holly rapped on the window as the bike's engine died to get Kristy's attention. Signaling a 'come here' wave at, she tried to smile, quickly making her way to the front door. Kristy smiled, sadly giving her a one armed hug at the door. Her other arm laden with a large dish, from which emanated a delicious aroma. "Hey chook, how are you doing?" She lifted one eyebrow and looked at Holly from under her eyelashes.

"You know? *Argh*, of course you know." She stepped back out of the door so Kristy could pass, bustling down the hall, with the covered dish.

"Holly, I think CNN knows." She rolled her eyes, smile thin lipped and cynical, striding past Holly and entering the kitchen. With a snort of derision she called back over her shoulder as Holly closed the door with a sigh of exasperation. "Masie was up at Marty' parent's place filling them in by eight this morning."

Holly joined Kristy in the kitchen. Kristy unwrapped a dish filled with fresh battered fish and chips. The aroma set Holly's mouth to watering. "I betcha ten bucks you haven't eaten." Kristy turned to her, one hand stuck on her hip, a questioning look on her face.

"No, I haven't. My belly is starting to complain. In the endeavor to take my mind off the mess of my life, I started on the mess in the spare room."

"Oh, awesome. Find anything interesting?"

"I found sheets and blankets. I have no idea who they belong to. I didn't get to the trillion boxes and the large cupboard yet."

"Well, I'll give you a hand if you want. Just give me a shout. Where are your plates?"

Holly passed her two dishes and dug out some cutlery. "Where's Marty?

I hope you left him some dinner."

"Yeah, he's up at his parent's house, holding his mother down. She's ready to hunt old Masie down." Kristy roared with laughter. "Cora apparently told Masie to take her broken arse home." She leaned on the kitchen bench with one hand and held her belly with the other, tears of laughter rolling down her face. "Cora's about ten years older than Masie, the most devout woman I know, and I've never heard a foul word come out of her mouth. Of course as soon as Cora was done putting a flea in Masie's ear, she came right down to our house to let us know. She was so furious, she was spitting tacks." Kristy wiped the tears of mirth from her eyes and sighed. "God, if they were all like that old sweetie, the island wouldn't have a grapevine worth two cents. For a mother-in-law, she's a keeper."

"I just can't understand why people listen to rubbish like that at all." Holly watched Kristy as she shared out the meal, her mouth watering. She gratefully accepted a full plate. Kristy shrugged and frowned as they sat down at the table to eat.

"Small community I guess. Everyone knows everyone's business, and it gets boring, they embellish to make it more interesting." Kristy popped a morsel of fish into her mouth and chewed. "It's kind of like Chinese Whispers. You either play the game, or you don't. Masie plays, Cora doesn't. Masie should have known better than to try and tittle-tattle her spiteful story to her." Sighing deeply, Kristy shrugged. "You just learn to ignore it after a while."

"Ugh. I don't know if I can, especially since I seem to be the center of attention—again."

Holly's belly grumbled a reminder and she tasted the lightly battered fish, twisting her face into a parody of ecstasy. "Oh this is good, Kristy. Usually I'm halfway through a tub of double chocolate ice cream in a disaster this huge."

"Caught this morning. Can't get fresher than that. Better than a chocolate fix any day." Kristy waved her empty fork at Holly. "So, the grain of truth in the gossip is you, Jack, and Masie got into a God-awful fight last night. Right?"

Holly looked down, pushed the fish around her plate for a few moments. Even though she was hungry and the fish was the best thing she'd tasted in a long time, her appetite was fast disappearing, again. "God-awful is an understatement. Masie told Jack and I that we could be half brother and sister, and basically called me a whore."

Kristy's mouth dropped open, her eyes widening in horror. "Oh, the wicked old woman. What did she do, look through the window and take notes while Celeste and James made out?"

Holly snickered. "I could see her doing just that. I don't know, Kristy. Every time I talked to James he spoke about Mum with nothing but respect. He had nothing but nice things to say about her, and her writing. It just didn't seem right—the idea of them together *that* way."

"What are you going to do about the old fella? Even if at the worst—the very worst he's your father, you can't ignore him. He was your mother's friend."

"What I have been doing I suppose. Visit with him every day, just like usual. He's a sweet, old guy. He enjoys the company—even when it's not a great day with his Alzheimer's." Holly got up to grab a bottle of wine out of the fridge and two glasses. She needed the time to think more about Kristy's question.

*The only reason I have for not visiting with James, isn't the fear of bumping into Masie. I can deal with that crabby old shrew. I'm not sure about seeing Jack again.* Grabbing a cork screw out of the drawer she rejoined Kristy at the table, popping the cork from the wine bottle and pouring them both a healthy glass. She smiled wryly. *How easy it would be, to drown my sorrows in this whole bottle.*

"Well, he could be my father for God's sake. *If* the rumor is true. If not, he's just a man who my mother used to go and see to confide in about her writing. Either way it can't hurt visiting the old guy. If for nothing more than my own selfish reasons of making myself feel good." *Well it sounds good, even to me. Pity it also means if James is my father, I've lost Jack.* Tears prickled at the back of her eyes and she blinked them quickly away. One thing she learned in foster care—never show your pain.

"You've got more guts than me, Holly." She twirled the stem of the glass in her fingers. "I think I'd be hiding away from the world."

Holly shook her head in disbelief. "No, not you, Kristy. I can't see you hiding under the bedclothes. You'd be doing the same thing as me." Sitting back in the hard backed chair, Holly puffed a mouthful of air between pursed lips. "I'm not going to turn tail and run just because some old woman has her underpants in a bunch. I came to Pitcairn for the truth, and either way, I'm going to find it. No one is going to stand in my way. If that means I find out that Jack is my half-brother—well, it means I've found family. That can only be a good thing—right?"

Kristy twisted her lips into a ghost of a smile. "I suppose. You two were so happy last night. It just doesn't seem right somehow."

The night at Kristy and Marty's felt like it had occurred eons ago. Since she found out about her real parents, murder, suicide, and Pitcairn nothing had seemed right in her world. *What is one more knife wound, learning that a man I was starting to fall in love with could actually be family? One more slice latticed across my heart.*

Holly thought she'd be able to control her emotions by now, but hot and wet, tears began to build in the corners of her eyes. She dropped her head back and stared at the ceiling, willing them not to fall. When she'd controlled herself and her defiant emotions, she stared at Kristy, and shrugged. "It is what it is. I have to deal with what I know."

"The Island Secretary's office is open tomorrow. Cheryl told me she's going to open the document safe and dig out the will. I can ditch the store and come with you if you like."

Holly appreciated the support, but she shook her head. "You've got work. I'll be fine." She toyed with the fork in her empty plate. "I'll go there, then head over to James to see him, before Jack gets home from work. I'm not looking forward to facing Masie again. She could quite happily rot in hell for all I care, but I have to see James. Jack—*him*, I don't think I could deal with yet."

"Well, you've got a friend in me, any time you want a shoulder to cry on, just let me know." Kristy patted her own slender shoulder with a twinkle in her eye and a twitch of a smile. "May look like a puff of wind will blow me over, but I can support a mate."

*Oh, God here comes the water works.* "Thanks, Kristy." Eyes downcast, Holly struggled not to break down again. "Thanks for everything, especially dinner."

Kristy got up and walked around the table, pulling Holly up into a tight hug. "You're my friend, and this is what friends do."

Holly, warm in Kristy's embrace, safe in her friend's arms, finally let the dam break.

# Chapter Thirteen

The island secretary's office was in a large building situated at the far end of the square. Sectioned off into three sets of offices, one was for the government treasury, one for the Post Office, and the other for council members, the mayor and the island secretary herself. The whole building was desperately in need of renovation—or a wrecking ball. Flaking paint and simple patch jobs covered holes and flaws in the building surround. Inside, the island secretary's office interior continued the grubby and decrepit theme. Painted walls looked as if they'd been painted over three or four times, and a dim, bare bulb, were a stark contrast with the furniture.

Crammed with modern desks, three against the wall on one side, three against the opposite side, printers and a large photocopier, the room was utilitarian and for a purpose. *I suppose it's not what it looks like, only what is required to get the job done.* Only two people sat in the bleak, dusty room, busy working behind humming computers.

A grey haired, bespectacled woman looked up, her glasses sliding precariously down on her nose. Pushing them back up onto the bridge of her nose with an impatient shove, she smiled. "Hi, you're Holly—after some documents are you?"

*Sometimes, it's nice everyone knows your business, saves having to explain yourself every five seconds.* Holly returned the smile and reached out to shake the portly woman's hand. "Yes, I'm Holly, you're Cheryl right? Kristy told me you were going to look in the office document safe for me."

Cheryl reached across the desk and squeezed Holly's hand in lieu of a handshake. "We don't much go for handshakes here lovey." She opened a drawer in her desk and rooted through the contents, head bowed to see into its depths, muttering under her breath. "Now, where did I put those darn keys?" Pushing up her glasses absentmindedly as they slid down her nose again, she cried, "A-ha!"

Dangling the small bunch of keys triumphantly in the air by its key ring, she clasped her hand around it with a smile. "Don't really use these things much. Knock on wood." She rapped at the wooden desk with her knuckles. "Only keep the wills in the safe, so it's opened very rarely. Either putting a new one in or taking one out." She groaned with effort as she heaved herself out of her chair and shuffled round the desk. "These old bones of mine'll be the death of me." She complained.

The tall, sandy haired man in the desk opposite Cheryl's snorted, choking down a laugh. "Oh stop complaining woman, I saw you out in the garden yesterday. You were going ten to the dozen with an adze, digging up a new row to plant some more vegetables. Nothing wrong with you."

Cheryl shot him a pained look. "You're half my age, Brian. I'm allowed to have a few gripes." She nodded at Holly. "I'll just go get that envelope." Cheryl disappeared through an open doorway into a windowless room at the back of the main office. Holly giggled behind her hand as Cheryl continued muttering under her breath, about cheeky young men half her age, and Brian rolled his eyes, leaning back in his padded office chair with a smile.

Rocking forward in his chair, Brian stood, leaning over his desk, and offered his hand to Holly. "I'll do the handshake thing." He laughed. "I'm Brian, the mayor. You're after your parents last will and testament I understand."

"Yes, I've been told there was one lodged here."

"Well, if there is, Cheryl will have it."

"I'm also trying to find out what happened to all their personal belongings. There are things in the house, packed in boxes, but, I'm not sure if they're my parent's things, or if they were left behind by the last tenants. It's hard to know who's they are..." Holly's voice trailed off as Brian frowned, eyebrows drawn together with concern.

"You've opened up boxes?"

"No, just some bags of sheets and towels." Holly was taken aback. Brian looked as though he'd been sucking on lemons. His mouth was so tightly pinched.

He stuck his nose in the air with a sniff, face reddening. "You really shouldn't have touched anything until you'd found out who had possession." He sat back down in his chair, rolling a pen between his hands, mouth twitching with irritation. "Same thing goes with the will I'm afraid. Cheryl can't just hand it over to anyone, willy-nilly, even on Pitcairn there are processes in place for official documents, young lady. You'll have to wait until the island magistrate reads it and finds out who the executor is."

Holly couldn't believe it. *One step forward, and two steps back.* "Okay, So when *can* I have the will? What about the stuff in the house?"

"Until you know who they belong too you shouldn't touch them." He nodded with self-importance, smug smile creasing his face.

"But, that's ridiculous. The boxes were left in *my* house. How can I know who they belong to, if I can't open them to see what's inside?"

Brian sighed and rolled his eyes in frustration. "Simple, young lady. Talk to the Young's. If it's not theirs, call the island police to oversee the opening. As for *your* house —how do you know what the will says? Your parents might have left the house to charity or instructed for it to be destroyed for all I know—for all *you* know. Do yourself a favor, and at least *try* to protect yourself from accusations later. You've got enough tongues wagging on the island already."

Holly, stunned, could do nothing but stand in front of him, slack-jawed with shock. *Okay, I may have misunderstood the process here, but this man is a complete creep. It seems like he's going out of his way to be uncharitable and nasty.*

Cheryl bustled back into the room carrying a thick yellowed envelope, mouth carved into a thin slit, eyes glittering. "Brian, for heaven's sake, that's enough. I know for a fact your parents taught you better manners than that." She slid behind her desk and thumped the envelope onto the desktop, ignoring Brian's glare from across the office.

"Cheryl, I'm the mayor. You shouldn't be speaking to me like that!" He spluttered.

"Mayor, my foot! You're my nephew, and I can speak to you how I like." She frowned. "Especially when you're acting like a snotty little kid. Have some respect for another Pitcairner. Her parents may have died a long time ago, but this is still extremely hard for the girl. Look at her face, for goodness sake. She looks like you've just slapped her."

*Oh, I think I like this woman.* Holly struggled to hold back an impromptu round of applause for Cheryl, settling instead, for a grin as she turned her back on the steaming, red headed man.

Peering over her glasses at Holly, Cheryl smiled kindly. "Ignore him. He can be a pain in the backside." She sat down in her chair with a groan and rolled herself in close to the desk. "There are two envelopes here actually." She slipped a rusted paper clip off the end of the large sachet, freeing a thin envelope that had been nestled close behind.

Holly eagerly moved to stand in front of her desk, a bubble of hope growing in her belly. "This one has your name on it Holly. It's not a legal document. It's been added separate from the will. This you can have. " She indicated the larger yellowed package, "This one I'll hand to the magistrate."

"Do you know what's in this one, or who it's from?" Holly asked as Cheryl passed her the smaller envelope, spidery writing spelling out 'Holly Christian.' It was light, and thin, suggesting only one or maybe two sheets of paper inside.

Cheryl shook her head. "I don't know love. I didn't have the Island Secretary job when either envelope was placed in the safe. Although we do have processes to follow," she looked down her nose across the room at Brian. "There is no register for wills, or other documents that were placed in the safe." She paused as she peered at the writing on the envelope. "It does look like Celeste's writing though."

"It's none of your business either, *Auntie*." Brian snapped from behind Holly. She glanced over her shoulder at him with raised eyebrows. *What a horrible little man.*

Cheryl sniffed and swatted his comment away like a pesky fly. Lowering her voice, she leaned in to speak in a quieter tone to Holly. "Look love, don't you worry. Not everyone here has the same narrow views as Masie, or my nephew."

Cheryl shot a quick glance across at Brian, then wrote something quickly on a piece of paper, folding it and slipping it across the table to Holly with a short nod.

She raised her voice. "I'll tell you what I'll do. I'll ring Matthew Young, and see if he left any junk at your place when they moved out. If they did I'll tell him to pop down and collect it. Otherwise ring Margaret, she's the island police woman, and get her to come down and witness you opening up the boxes. That should cover you from any wagging tongues."

Cheryl winked at Holly as she picked up the clandestinely written message, and tucked it out of sight behind the envelope.

"Thanks Cheryl."

Holly nodded politely at Brian, and escaped the office as quickly as she could, tucking note and envelope into the bottom of the basket she'd slung over her shoulder.

The square was busy this morning with both the Post Office and Government Treasury open for business, the locals gathering there and seated along benches that lined the plaza. Curious glances and whispered comments followed her as she hurried past, but she had no time or the inclination to worry now. *Talk all you want, I'm finding out slowly who really matters, who really cares.*

Out of the sight of the inquisitive crowd, she dug out the note, her hands shaking with a mixture of dread and excitement. Holly held the folded piece of paper for a moment just looking at the haphazardly folded missive. *What are you scared of? That you'll find out that Brian's your father?* Holly snorted with laughter. *It couldn't possibly get any worse.*

With trepidation still gnawing at her gut, Holly unfolded the note. Scrawled untidily across the paper were the words: 'I helped pack up your parents things. I'll come over this afternoon to see you.'

Holly crumpled it into her hand, heart beating hard with excitement. *At last, finally I might find out something about my parents that's not tangled in lies or innuendo. I might finally be able to find my mother's books. Cheryl might even be able to tell me what really happened, why my father did what he did.*

Knowing something precious was sitting in her basket waiting to be read, and curious to find out if it had indeed been written by her mother, Holly rushed to the store to pick up supplies. After she had dropped those at home, she still wanted to visit with James this morning. *Before Jack gets home from work.*

Reaching the checkout, Kristy waited to serve her, bouncing on her heels in excitement. She searched Holly's face with curious eyes. "So— did you go and see Cheryl?"

"Yup, got a little more than I bargained for too."

Kristy looked up from the can of beans she'd been scanning. "What?"

Looking around at the other customers perusing shelves, and still others in line behind her Holly shook her head. "Not here. There's a will, but it has to be opened by the magistrate to see who the executor is. There is something else, but there are too many ears." Holly lowered her voice, jerking a thumb at the curious listeners behind her.

Kristy grimaced and continued scanning items, slipping the groceries into Holly's basket. "Yeah, big ears and waggling tongues."

Holly stifled a snort of laughter, cupping her hand over her mouth.

"You off to see James this morning then?"

"Of course." Holly could feel the person behind her leaning in closer to listen. "After I've dropped off these groceries."

"Right-o, I'll pop in this afternoon."

"Make it late—I'll have a visitor."

Kristy raised one eyebrow and looked over Holly's shoulder. "Bert! You nosy old bugger! Lean in any closer and you'd be breathing down the woman's neck."

A gruff voice behind her coughed and grumbled, "Cheeky wench. Weren't doing nothing." Holly looked behind her to see a chastened, red faced old man. His nose hairs longer than the wispy white tufts attached around his ears, bald, age-spotted head reddened with embarrassment. He moved one foot in circles on the floor, eyes downcast. "Just think it's nice ha gal got the time for an old man, is all."

Holly giggled. The man looked like a chastened toddler, complete with pout. "Thank you, Bert. James is a sweet heart. He knew my mother, and sometimes he remembers and tells me things that I would never have known about."

Bert stared at her shyly, "Yous a good lass. Town's been talking, but don't concern ya-salf child." He nodded sagely. "Yorley remind them of your mother. Spitting image is you."

"I can't help that, but a little talk is not going to stop me from visiting James."

"Good on ye, love."

Kristy cleared her throat, and Holly turned back to the counter where Kristy stood with a fond smile. "You're all ready Holly." She took Holly's money and handed her back her change with a wink. "Give me a call when your visitor is gone, Holly."

With a nod and a smile, Holly left as Kristy called out to Bert. "Come on then, you old softy—gimme your groceries then."

# Chapter Fourteen

"Oh, it's you."

Masie stood in the doorway at James and Jack's house, feet planted slightly apart, arms crossing her breasts. She was not happy. She'd quickly covered a surprised expression upon opening the door, with a withering glare, mouth twisted into a tight lipped frown of disdain.

"Yorley really shouldn't be here."

"Why is that, Masie?" *There's no way you're pushing me away lady. Not now.*

Masie raised one eyebrow, and smirked, she wasn't moving an inch. "Yorley know why, you're not welcome here no more."

"That's lovely, Masie. First you insinuate that James is my father, then you refuse my admittance to his house." Despite quivering like a jelly inside, Holly maintained a cool exterior. Voice low, speaking in a conversational tone, she kept her calm, her fisted hands the only indication she wasn't as cool as she looked.

"Jack wouldn't like et that yous here."

Holly sighed, smiled serenely. "Well, that's just not true, and you and I both know it." *I don't even know if Jack would expect me to visit anymore. At least I know he's definitely not here.* Holly had seen the vacant parking spot on her way up the drive, but just because the bike wasn't there, didn't mean a thing. "Look, Masie, you can stand there as long as you like. The reason you don't want me coming in is because *you* don't like me, or have some imagined slight against my mother. Well, that's too bad. I'm not here for you, Jack or anybody else. I'm coming in to see James, and that's all there is to it."

Holly ignored the sharp intake of breath from the indignant woman, and pushed past her. James was in his usual spot in the recliner, gospel music playing on the TV. At Holly's entrance he looked up, eyes lighting up to see her. He fumbled with the remote control in his hands. "Argh. Damn nuisance of a contraption. Come here and turn ha damn thing down please."

Despite her nerves, Holly grinned and took the remote from him, turning the volume down to a level where they might be able to talk. "How are you doing, James?"

She sat on the edge of the padded armchair opposite James, hands relaxed in her lap, and watched him carefully. He seemed calm, lucid this morning, eyes bright. As Holly sat before him in what she hoped was a manner as calm as his seemed, she hoped he did not get an inkling of how she really felt inside. She was jittery, as if she'd stuck her finger in an electrical socket. Nerves twanged, and she felt as coiled up as a snake waiting to strike. *Nervous because of Masie? Nerves because Jack may come back early? Excited because an envelope with her name on it sat on the kitchen bench at home unread?* She supposed it was a mixture of all.

"You look good this morning."

Masie had taken her position in her favorite chair. Her arms seemed permanently clamped across her chest, a frown knitted in concrete disapproval on her for head. "He es good. Don't trouble him."

"Geez, woman, you're grumpy this morning. Both you and Jack must have gotten out of the wrong side of bed." James twisted around to stare at the ill-tempered woman. He sniffed and creakily turned back to Holly, "Jack slammed out of here like a madman this morning, disappeared all day yesterday. I don't know what's wrong with the pair of them."

The heat rose in Holly's face at the mention of Jack's name, and James leaned forward unblinking, mouth twitching in the corners. "Something's not right between you two."

"No, something's not right at all, James. That's why I'm here."

*I have to ask. If James seems to think Jack and I as a couple is normal, he can't think he's my father.* She eyed Masie, her face set in an unreadable neutral mask. She stared back, eyes narrowing at the distasteful old woman.

*I can't let this go on, this gossip, innuendo. The only one who can tell me for sure is sitting right in front of me.* She wavered for a minute, the words at the tip of her tongue. *Am I being selfish?* Holly shifted in her chair, uncomfortable with risking hurting the man, yet desperate for her own answers. "James? Was there something going on between you and my mother? I was told there was...an affair."

The old man rocked back in his chair, hands fluttering to his face. "Why would you say such a thing child?"

Holly's eyes flicked to Masie and James followed the glance. His mouth dropped open. "Masie?"

Masie leapt out of her chair, wild-eyed and furious. "Yorley have no right to ask hem such impertinent questions! You is a whore! Just like yous mother. Get out! Get out of this house!

James pushed himself out of his chair, staggered to his feet. He pointed a shaking finger at the old woman. "Masie! Yorley won't speak that way to ha gal. Celeste...wasn't no...whore." His breath hissed on the last word, he stumbled back and fell heavily into his chair.

Holly leapt to her feet, attention riveted on James. Masie was ranting and raving, but Holly could not understand She'd faded to a indistinguishable roar. She only had eyes for the old man. He had gone pasty white, sweat popping out in beads on his forehead, a haunted look in his eyes as he focused on Holly. "Celeste was everything to me, she was special. I loved her very much. She needed my help and I gave it. That's what was going on."

Tears, fat and glistening rolled down the James' cheeks and he pressed his hand hard to his chest. He leaned forward, mouth stretched in a gruesome toothy snarl, grunts of pain puffing through gritted teeth. Panic rose in Holly's belly as James seemed to fold in on himself, mouth becoming slack, eyes growing hazy.

Holly scrambled to catch him as James rolled forward, dangerously close to collapsing out of his recliner. "Masie!" She screamed, panic lacing through her body, voice thick with tears of shock. "Call the doctor. Call Jack!"

Masie towered above her as Holly struggled to hold the old man, pulling him down to lay his limp body flat on the wooden floor. "You did this! You killed him!" She screeched, spittle flying from her mouth, eyes wide open in fearful rage.

"Just make the calls, Masie. It's not too late." *Oh, please don't let it be too late!* Hands icy cold with fear, Holly grabbed a pillow of the recliner and slipped it under his head as the distraught, older woman took off at a run. James eyes opened, and he groaned, retched, hand gripping his chest. "Hurts," he whispered.

Holly leaned over him, tears dripping onto his gnarled and pain twisted face. "I know, I'm sorry. I'm so sorry." She stroked his hair, sobs racking her body as she watched him struggle to breath.

"Not...Celeste..." He reached up, grabbing at her shirt and pulling her down. His voice barely a whisper, he put his mouth to her ear. "Never. Celeste. She stopped me...affair...Not her."

James hand dropped from her shirt. A breath rattled from deep within his chest...then no more.

Holly looked into James' now serene face through a curtain of tears. "No, no, no, no..."

She put her head to his chest and listened, prayed for a heartbeat. *Nothing.*

A keening, a wailing began in the room and she placed her hands on his chest. With every thrust of CPR, the wailing noise became louder, echoed, competing against the cheerful gospel music, jarringly loud in Holly's panic filled mind.

Masie shrieked from the doorway, and ran to James side, slapping Holly hard across the face, pushing her away.

"Don't you touch him! You did this! Don't you dare touch him! You shut up your screaming noise, you killed him." She collapsed across James prone body, wailing, and tears falling, dampening his shirt.

Holly scuttled backward across the floor until she hit the wall, chair, something. The keening stopped short as the breath puffed out of mouth with the shock of impact with something hard against her back.

*Oh, my God. That was me*, she thought blankly. She stared unseeingly at the woman crouched over the man lying on the floor, shaking with sobs, wailing with loss. Holly curled up her legs, clamping her arms around them tight, laid her head on her knees and shut her eyes against the pain. Darkness descended, remembrance began.

\* \* \* \*

*Her heart beating fast in her chest, she scrambled out of the hiding place, banyan tree branches scraping at her back, getting caught in her hair. She felt and saw nothing, just needing to escape the darkness. Jack called out, his manic exit from the hidey-hole, noisy behind her, leaves scrunching and crunching under his hands and knees. "Holly, wait!"*

*Holly ignored him and began running down a leaf strewn path toward her house. Breath loud in her ears as she panted, air squeezing painfully from her lungs. A hand grabbed her by the back of the shirt, drawing her up short, and she struggled against the restraint. "Holly, I called for you to wait."*

*Holly looked up into his face as she bit her lip, eyes dry now, just wanting to get home. Something was wrong, something was very wrong.*

*"I'm coming with you. So slow down, stupid." His eyes, wide with fear, belied the insult.*

*"Okay. Just hurry. I gotta go home."*

Jack grabbed her hand and they walked quickly down the path together, both silent and deep in their own thoughts.

"What were they shooting?"

"I don't know; Goats, maybe wild chickens. When we get to your place, let me go first, okay?"

"No."

"You're so stubborn!"

"You're not so smart, Jack. Just because you're seven, doesn't mean you know everything..."

The pair burst out of the banyan tree patch, still arguing. Holly suddenly wished she'd listened. She wished she'd never left the space under the banyan trees at all. Her legs trembled, knees knocking as she stared at a tableau of horror.

Her father, back against a banyan tree, sat slumped, slanted on a dangerous lean, a large gun between his knees. That weapon had taken her daddy's face away, a bloody stump left in its place, blood, bits in the tree branches and the trunk of the ancient tree.

Jacks voice shrill and horror filled, tugging again at her shirt. "Don't look! Don't look, Holly, Oh, no!" The sound of retching as he threw up behind her, coughing, moaning with terror. "I'm running for Dad." Jack said, face ashen, wild-eyed with panic, he grabbed her hand and started to drag her away. "Come on, you can't stay here now."

Holly began to scream, beating at his hands with her small fists. "You leave me alone, Jack Quintal! I'm staying, I'm staying..."

Jack stopped in his tracks and grabbed Holly's shoulders, shaking her with all of his might. Her head wobbled on her neck, her hair whipping around her face. Holly struggled against him as he shouted at her. "There's nothing you can do. You can't stay here alone with them." A string of snot mixed into the tears that ran unchecked down his face and he swiped at his nose with his sleeve, pushing the snot into a silvery stream across his face. Holly pushed against him with all her might and he let go without warning. She fell, rolled over and over and landed flat out in the grass, face down into the carefully mown front lawn.

"I'm going to get my Dad!" Jack's voice broke as Holly heard him start to run. His footsteps fading in the quiet.

Holly lay still for a second, the itch of the grass scratching her wet cheek. She sat up, pushing at the hair falling around her face, dirt gritty on the wetness of her skin. She felt nothing. She looked past what was her father, that thing with her daddy's shirt and *shorts, his bare feet splayed in opposite directions, looking for her mother.*

*She was there, on the ground, not far from the thing that looked like her daddy. Lying flat on the ground, one leg straight, the other curled up underneath her. Her dress was pulled up around her middle, so Holly pulled the hem down to cover her knickers. Mummy always told her never to let the boys see her knickers. "I fixed it, Mum, it's okay," she whispered. She stroked her mother's hair and smiled, she looked so pretty, blond hair spread like a halo around her head.*

*There was nothing she could do about the hole in her chest. It had made a big mess, Mum's dress was torn, the top spilling open, her bra and strap there for all the world to see. Holly tried to cover her up, but, there wasn't enough material to pull up without it pulling back and opening up further. It worked if she put her mother's slack hand on her chest, to cover the hole, the red stuff — blood—that stained everything. Some came off in Holly's hand and she wiped it on her shirt, wiped, wiped, wiped her hand furiously, tears of frustration as her hand became clean, but her shirt became stained. "Don't be mad, Mum," she whispered. "I tried to help, but I made my shirt dirty instead."*

*She lay down beside her mother, she was warm and sticky, but Holly knew she wouldn't care if Holly was only close to her. She lay next to her mother just as she used to do when Holly had to go to bed, tucking herself into the hollow between her chest and her arm. Her mother's arm was loose to the side. Now, there was no arm hugging her close, but she hugged her mother close instead. Clamping her own hand up and around her mother's neck. She stuck her thumb in her mouth. Mum had her eyes closed, she couldn't see to tell her not to, and she squeezed her eyes shut too.*

*The dark was better sometimes. Sometimes being able to see meant you hurt.*

# *Chapter Fifteen*

Holly opened her eyes. She was in her own bed Kristy sat in a chair by her bedside, book open in her lap. Kristy's eyes were damp and she stared unfocused at the novel she held. Holly recognized the book straight away, her mind grasping at anything, but the sorrow written clearly on Kristy's face. *It's one of mine, can't be enjoying it much... Oh, no...no...James...*

"Kristy."

Kristy shut the book with a snap as she jumped. "Oh, Christ. You gave me a fright. You okay?"

"Yeah. James?"

Kristy's mouth twisted down, face crumpling, her eyes red and raw. She sobbed. "He's gone, chook. I'm so sorry." She came and sat on the edge of the bed as Holly's shoulders began to shake, tears to fall.

"It's my fault, I upset him again. I confronted himMasie...It was horrible." Holly sat up—a little too fast. Her head spun and black spots danced before her eyes. Grabbing a handful of tissues from beside the bed she blew her nose noisily. Holly tried to speak, the lump in her throat choking her.

Clearing her throat, Holly's voice was not her own, weak and wavering. "He died right in front of me; trying to convince me he didn't have an affair with my mother. Oh, poor Jack!" Holly burst into a fresh round of tears at the thought of Jack losing his father.

"Holly, James was an old man. He had a bad heart. He was suffering a hateful disease. He lived a long and healthy life until now. Jack's hurting, but he's just as concerned about you. He told me to ring once you woke up. We had to get the doctor to sedate you." She swept Holly's hair back from her face and looked carefully into her eyes. "You were in shock. No one could get through to you, you were wrapped up tight and not responding. It was scary, Holly. Jack was bouncing from hysterics over his father to concern with your well-being."

Sitting upright in the bed had made her feel dizzy and weak, and she leaned back against the headboard. "I still don't feel right making a distressing situation even worse for Jack." Holly put her head in hands, shame heating her cheeks. "Poor Jack." She lifted her head out of her hands as another thought occurred to her. "What's happening with James?"

"The funeral's at six tonight."

Holly stared, mouth slack with shock. "Today? He only just..."

"I know, love, but that's how it has to be here. No mortuary, no way to look after the body. They've been getting the graveside ready and making a coffin all afternoon. Do you feel up to coming?"

Holly looked down at her hands which tore nervously at the tissues she held. The guilt she felt told her it wasn't right for her to show her face, but her conscience told her it was wrong not to go. "Yeah. I have to say goodbye. Not only to James, but to my parents I think too." Holly looked into Kristy's questioning face. "When James died, it triggered more memories." She sobbed, pain of loss threefold. "I remembered finding my parents outside my house... both..."

"Oh God, Holly. No wonder we found you in the state we did." Kristy put a hand to her mouth in horror. "Do you honestly think you should go then?"

"I have to. I've finally remembered. Not only losing James, but how I felt losing my parents. I remember everything now. My mum singing in the kitchen as she made my breakfast, tucking me in to bed at night. My dad—he had a nickname for me—Curly." Holly wiped at her eyes with the shredded tissues. "I remember." She shook her head against the wave of memories, her parents smiling at her, at each other. Hiding as her parents argued, laughing as they cuddled in the kitchen. *At least there were good times I can hang on to—good memories.*

Kristy hugged her tight. "I'll be there for you, Chook, but right now I have to go home and get ready, and see if Marty's home from the Edge. He went down to help make the coffin. If it's okay, I'll ring Jack, let him know you're alright."

"Tell him I'm sorry."

Kristy rubbed her back and stood to leave. "Tell him yourself, he's not angry at you, more worried than anything else." She picked up her book and slipped it into her bag, slinging it over her shoulder. "I'll be back for you at half past five."

* * * *

Holly stood straight backed, feet together, hands clasped at the graveside. Dressed in the only black she had, a knee length skirt, and frilly shirt, she felt inappropriate both in dress and in her presence. No one had made her feel unwelcome at the service at the church, but she'd been getting some strange looks. *I can't care what people are thinking. I'm here for James and to support his family, to support Jack.* Kristy stood loyally to one side of her, every now and then shooting her a sidelong glance of concern. Whatever the doctor had given her this afternoon to make her sleep had continued to make her feel woozy and out of it. A few times Kristy had put a hand under an elbow to support her as she'd tottered dangerously close to collapse.

The crowd murmured as the pall bearers solemnly strode toward the yaw in the ground, parting to let the six men who carried James coffin on their shoulders. Jack walked as head pallbearer, the coffin resting on his right shoulder, tear stained face solemn, and mouth twisted downward. Holly put her fist to her mouth and bit her knuckle to prevent a loud sob, Kristy moved closer to slip an arm around her and pull her close.

A tearful community surrounded the graveside, and the coffin was placed on two makeshift poles laid across the grave. A Pitcairn flag draped across the coffin, and the pastor stepped forward to begin his final prayer. Holly bowed her head and closed her eyes against the sight, her heart breaking as she remembered the open coffin in the church.

The coffin was constructed of plywood, basic and measured for James height and weight. Locals had lovingly placed him inside, decorated the edges with native flowers, Frangipani, Hibiscus and sprigs of fern. Jack and James friends had tucked photos, mementos, and James favorite gospel DVD inside for his final destination. Every moment of the service had been fully devoted to James, his love of the sea and his island. Holly had found it more touching than any other funeral she'd attended before.

Head still bowed, Holly felt Kristy's arm drop from her waist, another replace it on the other side, and she glanced up to look into Jack's sad face. Her traitorous heart skipped a beat, and made her flush with shame. "Jack. I'm so sorry," she whispered.

"We'll talk later, Holly. I just need your support right now."

Holly nodded. His need and his trust that she'd be there for him, twisted the emotions swirling in her gut like a knife. *How could he want me to be there for him when I caused this?* A tear ran down her cheek as self-pity encroached on sorrow and she scrubbed it off her cheek like it had scalded her. *No, this is not the time for self-concern. It's Jack that needs me now.*

The pastor intoned the last rights as the posts supporting the coffin were pulled away, and it was lowered gently into the ground. Jack's hand tightened on her waist and a sob tore from his throat as the lid disappeared from sight. She wound her arm around his waist and hung on tight, responding to his urgent need. A final hymn was sung, tear stained and sweet, voices ringing in the quiet early evening, a Pitcairn staple, sung at all occasions—*The Sweet Bye and Bye.*

*There's a land that is fairer than day,*
*And by Faith we can see it afar,*
*For the Father waits over the way,*
*To prepare us a dwelling place there.*
*In the sweet (in the sweet)*
*By and by, (by and by)*
*We shall meet on that beautiful shore*
*In the sweet (in the sweet)*
*By and by, (by and by)*
*We shall meet on that beautiful shore*
*We shall sing on that beautiful shore*
*The melodious songs of the blest,*
*And our spirits shall sorrow no more*
*Not a sigh for the blessing of rest.*
*To our bountiful father above*
*We will offer our tribute of praise*
*For the glorious gift of his love*
*And the blessing that hallow our days.*

As the last strain of the hymn rang out over the crowd, every local, man, woman, and child took a turn to spade a load of red dirt into the grave, each saying a personal goodbye to James. As Holly took the spade from Kristy with a sad smile, she paused and closed her eyes, bowing her head. *So sorry James. It was truly an honor and a privilege to know someone who had such respect for my mother. Who showed me the greatest respect.* Holly dug her spade into the dirt and slowly drizzled the dirt onto the coffin below. "I'll miss you."

Returning to Jack's side Holly watched as the men finished filling the grave, not resting till the last spade full had been patted down. Dusk had fallen. The red and gold of the encroaching night streaked the sky. Jack cleared his throat. "Everyone is welcome back at the house. We'd like you all to come and remember Dad."

He looked down at Holly, eyes moist, voice soft. "We'll talk after everyone's gone."

Holly was surprised at the atmosphere at the house. It was packed with locals, all laughing, eating and chatting merrily. As she wound her way around, trying to find a space for herself and Kristy, Jack dealt with his guests. Snippets of conversation she did hear, all involved James, his sense of humor, love of the water and the jokes he played on people. Tears and sorrow had been replaced with laughter and love as they remembered him. Holly couldn't have thought of a better way to celebrate someone's life.

Masie avoided both her and Jack, much to Holly's relief. Masie stood with Sarah at the graveside and gathered with her other cronies at James' house, all the while staring hatefully at them. Every time Jack touched Holly's hand, or slip a consoling arm around her waist, Masie would frown with distaste and bow her head to whisper to whichever sympathetic listener was nearby. To Holly's surprise, such things didn't bother her. James' last words still rung true in her mind, any last niggling doubts she had regarding her mother's so called affair with James had gone. *Masie could spit hateful words all she liked. It didn't mean they were true.*

Gradually the mourners departed, leaving just Kristy, Marty, Jack, and Holly behind. Kristy hauled a garbage bag out of the trash bin and tied it with a firm tug. "Well, that's the last of it, Jack."

Jack wiped his hands on a dish towel, and smiled. "Thanks, Kristy."

Marty took the trash bag and slid his free arm around Kristy's shoulders. "Come on love, let's head home." He jerked the bag. "We'll drop this at the end of the drive, mate. Rubbish day tomorrow."

Kristy hugged Holly, then Jack. She growled as she squeezed him as hard as she could, then pulled back to look into his eyes. "So sorry, Jack. He was a good man."

"I know."

Marty hugged Jack, adding a manly clap on the back. "Hang in there, mate. Come up for a beer." The big man cleared his throat, and knuckled at his eyes. "He was like a second father to me, Jack."

Eyes puffy with emotion, Jack nodded, the two men smiling sadly at each other. Kristy tugged at Marty's hand, and slipped an arm around his waist, looking up at him with a sad smile. "Come on, Marty. Let me take you home."

Jack walked them to the door, Holly following. They said their sad good-byes, and then closed the door gently behind them.

They stood looking at each other, the first time they'd been alone since that awful night. Holly wanted to go to him, hold him tight. Unsure about how he felt after she'd pushed him away with such decisiveness, she felt frozen in place. He leaned back against the door. "I have something to show you, but before I do, I need you to listen."

"Okay, Jack."

He motioned to the lounge. "Wait there. I'll be back in a sec."

The lounge was an empty shell without the hordes of mourners, and without James in his favorite chair. Holly could feel the loss of him, cold in her heart, but she could almost hear his voice, gruff with laughter. 'I'll be darned if you be sad over me." She smiled as she thought fondly of his gruff exterior, his soft heart.

Jack sat beside her with an old shoe box, crumpled with age in the middle and tied with a frayed piece of string. "What's in here erased any doubt for me, and will for you. But, Holly, I always knew there was something good between us—something pure. Nothing a vicious, old woman, with an agenda, could tear apart."

He pulled at the string, opening the box and searched through the box, which held papers, and booklets, pulling out five old passports. He held them in his hand and stared at Holly, eyes soft and hopeful. "I rang Brett. He figured out there was no way we could be brother and sister." He looked down at the passports, then put them and the box on the coffee table in front of them. Turning to Holly he held her hands tight in hers and looked deep into her eyes, searching for acceptance.

"The dates confirm it. Dad wasn't even on island when you were conceived—not for two months before you possibly could have been conceived, and six months after."

The last nagging doubt she'd had fell away as her heart lifted, and tears of joy beading in her eyes. "Oh, Jack."

He smiled. "I love you, Holly. You know it's true, and tonight I need you more than ever. Will you stay with me? Just be with me, hold me? I just...don't think I could be alone tonight."

Holly threw herself into his arms and held him tight. *Tell him. Tell him you love him too goddammit!* She couldn't form the words she knew deep inside were true, and her mind rebelled at the thought. Her mouth refused to voice the thought. *Everyone I love gets taken away*, she reasoned. *I love him so much. I can't lose him again.* She sobbed at her own impotence. "I honestly thought you'd hate me. Hold me responsible for your father..."

"Why? Dad was ill. He had been for a very long time. If anything your visits brought him a few hours of happiness every day." He laughed softly. "Even when he was having a bad day, your presence was to him, just like he had Celeste back. I know that's strange to think about, but your mother brought him joy too."

He pulled back out of her tight embrace, sweeping her hair away from her face, cupping her chin. "Will you stay?"

"Only if you kiss me first, Jack."

He kissed her. He bent his head and claimed her mouth with a tender loving touch, lips caressing, mouth teasing. Letting her take the lead, but showing her how much he wanted her, needed her, sorrow wending through every tender touch.

She kissed him, mouth moving to accept his request, heart clamoring, responding to his love, pressing in for more. Her mouth demanding passion, relief, love, transmitting through every breath, every sigh. Compassion for his loss, tinting every loving caress.

They kissed each other, arms weaving around each other's bodies, into each other's hair, passion blind, letting sensory pleasure take control. Pulling tighter, mouths hungrily accepting, gasps as the pressure intensified, mouths parted, tongues delved, tasted, desperation as close just wasn't close enough.

Reluctantly they parted, Jack switching off lights as they walked through the house, until they reached his room. Moonlight stippled the room, as they faced each other, inches apart. One step and she was in his arms, no words needed, kisses doing all the talking. Jack stripped off his shirt, dropping it to the floor, lifting her frilly shirt over her head to join it. Her hair swinging messily to lie golden in the moonlight down her back.

Holly gasped as skin touched skin. Jack's mouth lowered to her neck, nipping and tasting her neck, leaving a trail of fire that ran from her heart, beating out of control, to the very core of her belly. Jack slipped off a bra strap with one finger, as his mouth worked along a slender shoulder. She reached up behind her back to rid herself of the bra. She wanted to feel all of him against her—her nipples against the lace raw with aching.

He pulled it away with a groan and replaced it with his mouth, Holly's head dropping back at the shock of wet heat against aching breast. His tongue did dangerous twirls, every flick and tease sending lightning bolts to add to the throb between her legs. His mouth was suddenly everywhere, breast, hollow of her throat, fluttering across her jawline.

Her fingers splayed across his firm hairless chest, running around to his back to pull him close, the sensation of her nakedness against his smooth chest making her knees weak with lust. Her head dropped to his shoulder, burying her face into his neck, inhaling the faint scent of aftershave.

Jack's hands were in her hair, clutching handfuls of hair as he twisted her back to devour her mouth. Hot, out of control and deep, all tenderness gone, bruising with passion. His hands traveled down her back to the waistband of her skirt. With a moan that moved from her mouth to the very center of her body, he broke the kiss, and pushed the offending garment down to drop at her feet. With a feral growl, he picked her up in his arms and carried her to his bed, laying her on the moonlight dappled covers.

\* \* \* \*

Shucking off his pants and boxers he almost lost it right there, as he watched her writhe in passion on the bed, one hand clutching her throat, one at her breast, her eyes cloudy with lust. He could barely control his haste to join her there, his loins burning with the sight of her, all sense lost, only his need for her branded in his mind.

There was no more thinking as she parted her legs to grant him entry, spoke his name, told him *now*, cried out in ecstasy as he plunged deep within her warmth, her flesh greedily allowing him entrance, her slick, swollen core, her body arching to meet his. He shuddered as he buried himself to the hilt, and paused. She grabbed his hips, gyrated against him, almost sending him over the edge as he fought to control himself. With a whimper she said one word, "Please." He succumbed.

They rocked together, worlds colliding, heat exploding as they went over the edge as one.

# *Chapter Sixteen*

"Hi."

Holly opened her eyes, a dreamy smile playing on her lips. Jack lay on his side, head cradled in his hand, elbow resting on the bed, watching her with a matching slow smile, his naked body pressed up against hers.

"Hi, yourself." A tingle ran through her body as something lower down twitched against her leg, signaling that it too was awake.

A curl flopped onto his forehead, his brown eyes crinkling in the corners, a devilish smile tipping the corners of his mouth. He was something she definitely enjoyed waking up to.

He ran his hand up her body, leaving nerve ends popping and fizzing in its wake. "I've been lying here for ages, willing you to wake up."

She grinned. "You, or what's awake down there." Holly put her hand on the problem, making Jack close his eyes and rock back in pleasure.

"Both." He sighed. "I couldn't make up my mind which was more important. To wake you up so little Jack could have his way with you again, or wake you up so you'd stop snoring." He yelped when she squeezed him. "Hey, watch it." He laughed.

"You cheeky bugger." She hoisted herself up on her elbow and brought her hand up to the back of his head. "Now, kiss me until I forget you just insulted me."

Jack happily complied.

\* \* \* \*

"I keep thinking Dad's going to walk down the hall and ask for his breakfast." Jack joined Holly at the kitchen table, passing her a steaming mug.

"I know, Jack. I walked past the lounge expecting him to be in his recliner. It just seems oddly empty without him here." She reached across the table and squeezed Jack's hand. "I'm sorry."

Jack stirred and tipped the cereal in his plate with his spoon, eyes downcast. "Yeah, I suppose. I knew that I'd lose him one day. Just didn't think the day would come. Silly, huh?"

"No, no, not at all. When Bill and Tina died I still expected that usual Sunday morning phone call, or for Tina to walk through my front door with a new book she'd found, or a bag of donuts she'd bought from the bakery down the road. It leaves a space, nothing or no one can fill. It just gets easier to deal with, that's all."

"I know you're right." Jack sighed, his smile not quite reaching his eyes. "Thank you for staying with me last night. It was easier to wake up with you by my side." He turned his hand around in hers so they were palm to palm, squeezing back.

He cleared his throat. "So, what are your plans today?"

"Depends on what you're doing."

"I have to keep busy I think. I'm going to head into work—but will I see you after?"

"I'll cook dinner. I've got a few things to do myself." Which includes that letter sitting unopened on the bench at home, maybe call Cheryl, Kristy. So much was yet unanswered.

* * * *

Holly helped clean up, trying to keep Jack's mood light, distracting him with chatter. The house echoed without James there, leaving a hole even Holly knew she couldn't fill. A parent's loss, she knew all too well now. She knew there wasn't much she could do, but be there for him.

Holly kissed Jack goodbye at the doorstep, and started the walk home, her step light. With all the sadness over the last four days, and the loss of James still heavy on her heart, she wondered why her shoulders felt so unburdened. Was it because she'd remembered her parents finally? That she knew now there were good memories of them amongst the ones she wished she could forget? Was it because of Jack? She shook her head as she picked her way down the dirt road. She knew the sun seemed brighter, the smells of the hibiscus growing alongside the road smelled sweeter.

The roar of a bike behind her grew louder, put-putting and grinding as the rider changed down gears and pulled up beside her. Cheryl's smiling face peered down at her, the bike grumbling under her bulk. "Morning, love. Just heading your way. Jump on, I'll carry you the last few yards."

When they arrived at her house, Holly opened up the door, the stifling heat inside the house rushing back out at her. "Whew! I'll open up the house, and put the jug on Cheryl. Make yourself at home."

"Alright love, I'll open up the lounge for you. A closed up house here gets stuffy in this heat." She winked and smiled cheerfully. "Didn't think you'd go home last night. Jack looked pretty attached."

Holly did a double take, but Cheryl's face only showed an honest happiness for her. No sign that her comment was a spiteful dig at her spending the night with Jack. Cheryl, with her keen eye, noticed the surprised look and waved a hand at her. "Don't be shocked, lovey. We don't all have sticks up our bums' like some we could mention. I'm really happy for you and Jack. It's about time someone looked out for him for a change, made him happy instead of him running after everybody else."

Still smiling Holly walked through the house, opening windows. In the kitchen she threw open the door and heaved a sigh of relief as a gust of cool wind lifted the hair, sticky on her neck. Out of the corner of her eye she started as something fluttered then lifted on the gust of air, sliding along the counter top and disappearing over the edge. *The letter!* With a cry she rushed around the bench to the dining room.

It had slipped down between the breakfast bar and a small, glass door cabinet and she knelt down to reach underneath. With the tips of her fingers she pinched it out from under, swearing under her breath as something scratched sharp at her forearm as she dragged it back. A long red welt attested to the damage and she rubbed at it as it throbbed painfully.

"What the hell?" She looked back under the cabinet. A floor board was lifted out of alignment, a screw head sitting slightly up above the surface. *That's odd.* She looked at the floor boards at her knees. Tongue in groove, they were set at odds to each other and nailed in. *Why is that one screwed?* She peered back under the cabinet.

"What are you doing on the floor?" Cheryl's amused voice came from behind her.

"There's something weird under here." She scrambled to her feet and dusted off her knees, her heart beating fast with anticipation. "Give me a hand to move this cabinet, please?"

The two women took an end each and scraped the heavy cabinet away from the breakfast bar. In an oblong of dust where the cabinet had been sitting two sections of floor board were oddly out of place amongst the others.

"What on earth?" Cheryl said, puzzled expression lining her face. She pushed her glasses up her nose and bent down with a groan for a closer look, knees cracking loudly. She brushed the dust away with her hand. "You got a screwdriver?"

Holly was breathing hard with excitement. "No, I don't think so. Will a butter knife do it?"

"Should."

Holly's feet barely touched the ground as she ran to the cutlery drawer and yanked it open, knives, forks and spoons rattling with shock. Grabbing the flat edged knife, she hurried back and attacked the screw that had so brazenly scratched her, fingers shaking with eagerness. After fifteen minutes of struggling, the knife slipping, the sharp edge of the screw cutting her twice, Holly gave up with frustration. Throwing the knife down she sat down heavily on her heels. "This is so not working."

Cheryl looked down from her lofty spot on a chair she'd dragged over to watch the show. "Nope. Certainly ain't." She pursed her lips. "You sure you ain't got no screwdrivers?"

Holly's bark of laughter was tinged with disappointment. "I'm calling Kristy. Marty should have something."

Kristy laughed at the odd request when Holly phoned her. "Okay, but do you want flat-head, Phillips or a square head?"

Holly wailed with confusion. "Geez, there's a choice? The screw has a straight across mark in it."

"Okay, I'm coming down. I think you want a flat-head—but I'm bringing all three just in case."

Kristy arrived with a tool box, and armed with another chocolate cake. "Thought you'd need both." She said with a laugh.

Unable to keep her curiosity in check any longer, Holly relieved her of the tool box, and started to dig through the tools, looking for the right one for the job. Kristy and Cheryl looked on with amused grins, shooting sidelong looks at each other. Cheryl poked the air in Holly's direction, with a bemused expression. "I guess you're going to have to put on the jug, Kristy. Looks like Miss Fixit here has other things on her mind."

Holly laughed, without looking up from the toolbox, producing a screwdriver out of the box "Aha!" She scuttled over to the boards to resume the task, this time with the right tool at hand. It was one hundred times easier this attempt, much to her excitement. Four screws held in each board, all protesting strongly at being unscrewed. *Must have been like this for a while.* She wondered how long exactly.

She tuned out the noise of coffee being prepared just out of sight in the kitchen. The sound of Cheryl and Kristy talking faded to a dull hum as the last screw finally gave up and allowed its removal. Flipping the first, then the second board out of position, Holly hovered with anticipation over the hole it revealed. An oblong 'safe' had been created below. A thick layer of dust sat on top of another box, and Holly wiped it clean with her hand. On first glance, through the smears she'd wiped with her fingers, the colors, red, maroon and brown were instantly recognizable as the Pitcairn curio wood of choice. *The puzzle box, James told me about.* The excitement that had been curling in her belly, now exploded in twisting coils of hope.

"What is it?" Kristy's voice over her shoulder awoke her from her inner thoughts.

"I think it's the puzzle box James told me about."

There was not much room between the safes outer edges and the box. It had obviously been constructed to fit this item on purpose. Meant to hide this and this only. Holly managed to lever it out with her fingers and scrambled to her feet, clutching it in her hands.

The box had a film of dust on it so thick, wiping the surface with her hands didn't make much of a difference. The shape was odd. Oblong, flat on all sides except one, the top had a movable stick that slid out to the side. 'Celeste' was clearly wood burnt into the dust free space under the movable arm.

Holly sat, legs weak, in a chair next to the table and stared unseeingly at the box. *At long last she had a piece of her mother's life sitting in her lap. Something tangible to hold onto.* A tear rolled down her cheek and plopped into the dust on the box, staining it a dull black. Kristy, tutted sympathetically and came to stand next to her, rubbing at her back. "What's that for, Chook? You should be dancing a jig, not blubbering."

Holly smiled up into Kristy's face, eyes glistening. "Happy tears. Finally I have something of my mum's." She waggled the box. "Apart from this sliding bit on top, I have no idea how to open it."

Cheryl leaned forward in her chair and reached out her hand. "Give me a look, love? Me old man used to make these ages ago. They used to be all the rage with passengers on cruise ships. We could sell eight or nine of these on one ship alone."

Holly reluctantly passed over the box. *First the wait to open the safe, now a wait to open the box.* She smiled. *At least you knew how to make this interesting, Mum.* She watched as Cheryl turned the box over in her hands, a dull thump echoing from the box as she turned it end on end. It seemed as if Holly and Kristy both were holding their breath as Cheryl muttered aloud. "Okay... Yup...Alright."

Cheryl looked up, a gleam of satisfaction in her eyes, mouth twitching into a smile as she saw a captive audience. "Simple." Sliding the arm closed on the box, she turned it upside down and patted the bottom of the box till she heard a clunk. With a flourish, box still upended, she twisted the arm out again, and then slid it out completely. Turning the box over again, she slid the whole top off in the other direction, opening the secret compartment within. Handing Holly the three distinct pieces of the box, she said. "I expect you'll want to know how that works, but considering what's inside, I'd guess not right now."

Holly took the box with shaking hands and peered inside. A dark colored hard-cover book, diary sized was inside, 'Celeste Christian' written on the cover in the same spidery writing as on the envelope. Removing the diary and placing the box onto the table, Holly turned the book over and over in her hands. She then opened it, flipping through the pages. More than half the pages were crammed full of the same spidery hand writing. *Later. I'll read it later on my own.* She slipped the envelope in between the pages and closed the book, hugging it to her chest. Kristy and Cheryl looked at her expectantly. "You're not going to read it now, are you?" Kristy asked, voice tinged with disappointment.

Holly looked at her eager face and shook her head, laughing as Kristy's face fell. "No, but I'll fill you in. I think I need to have time to digest it."

Sighing, Kristy nodded. "I know. It's just that I'm just so curious I could bust. I understand though."

Cheryl coughed, cleared her throat. "I'm glad we found something of your mother's, because that's why I'm here."

The bubble of pleasure that Holly had been cocooned in deflated a little. *This didn't sound good.* "It's about when you helped pack up Mum and Dad's stuff, right?"

Cheryl nodded, her mouth pressed firmly together. She puffed a breath of air through, pushing up her glasses on her nose with a finger, avoiding direct eye contact. "You won't find much. If anything at all, love." She looked down at her hands which worked restlessly against each other in her lap. "Masie, Sarah, Hannah, and I cleaned up the house after you left the island. Sammy's mother, Hannah, took all his stuff with her." She paused and looked up at Holly, glasses steamed up in the corners from tears that had begun to fall. "Masie was crazy angry. All of Celeste's things that she could find, anything not screwed down…it went under the copper and was burnt. When the copper got too hot and begun to over-boil, she started a bonfire out the back on the lawn. She was storming in and out of the house. Clothes, books, toiletries—anything—on the fire. You couldn't talk to her. You couldn't hold her back. She had the strength of ten men. Sarah and I were screaming at her to stop, but it was like she was possessed."

Kristy grabbed a handful of tissues and passed it to the distraught woman, now heaving with sobs. She blew her nose, the sharp toot, echoing in the silent room. Holly sat frozen in her chair, as she imagined Masie's rampage through the house, crazy with the need to destroy anything her mother had touched.

"Why? Why would she do that to just Mum's things?"

"I don't know darling."

Holly could feel her mind slipping sideways, against more painful news. "James said Mum wrote in books…Did Masie burn—"

Cheryl sobbed, tears thickening her voice. "They were the first to go. She was half demented. Sarah was pulling at her arms, trying to stop her from throwing them on the fire, but Masie was out of her mind. She just wouldn't stop. She was getting rid of everything. She didn't burn everything…" Cheryl lifted her glasses to swipe at her eyes with the ball of damp tissues, and reached for her basket. Handing Holly a slip of paper, she said, "I saved this. It fell out of one of the books while Sarah and Masie were fighting. I hid it in my shirt." She smiled a watery smile. "I'm glad I did. I never told anyone I had it, not even my husband."

Holly opened the creased and age stained piece of paper. It was a poem, written in her mother's same scrawl, about Holly. Through a haze of tears she read. In her mind her mother's voice recited the words, and she knew she had been loved.

> The moment you were born
> My sweet, baby girl
> I held you in my arms
> My sweet, blue eyed girl
> My world, once had stopped
> Now re-evolved.

\* \* \* \*

> Your tiny fist in mine

My sweet, baby girl
Your sweet eyes locked on mine
My sweet, angel dear
A purpose to live my life
Just in your sweet, baby's breath

\* \* \* \*

If my cause was once lost
My sweet, baby girl
Is now ever found
My sweet, angel fair
My promise is to you
For love evermore

# Chapter Seventeen

*14th October*

*I've never written in a diary before, so I'm not sure how to start. Dear Diary? Today I did this? How do you start?*

*James says that when I write, all my emotions come out on the page. I have so many conflicting thoughts and feelings right now...He can see me whirling with them, struggling to focus. Write them down, Celeste. Write them down, he says.*

*He has this look on his face when he talks about my writing—a proud smile, something in his eyes. It reminds me of my father, that look when he taught me to tie my shoes, and I did that first perfect bow.*

*James makes me feel as if I can do anything. He prods and picks and corrects my spelling. Growls at my grammar mistakes and crosses out big sections of things in my books with his dreaded red pen...but when I get it right...his face glows with pleasure. He laughs at the right place, is sad when I've written it to be so...Is that what real writers feel? Do they sneak into libraries and watch the readers? Creep behind bookshop shelves and watch buyers peruse shelves? Wishing they'd pick up the book they'd spent days, months, years, agonizing over?*

*James says that one day my words can get us out of here, Holly and me. I don't think anything can though. He's wrong about that. Pitcairn is like mud, sucks you in and keeps you held in place—tough to get out of, and hard to wash off. There's no escape. Writing can, just for the moment, just for the space of a paragraph set me free. If I write, I'm where my character is, what he or she is feeling, involved in their plans, can* meddle in or correct their problems, make them cry, make them laugh. What happens when I'm stuck in real life...outside of my stories? My every day, normal me stuff? I just seem to make it worse. There's no one with a pen fixing my mistakes or writing my big finale—no escape from reality.

I have to hide if I want to write 'this nonsense' that takes up my time when I could be doing 'real work'. I need to make sure Sammy is going to be away —really away—so he doesn't sneak in and find me 'wasting my time'. So Diary, you're my secret, my escape, my friend. Be kind to me. Now James can't.

I miss him.

* * * *

16th October

James cornered me in the store—risky business. The rumors circling about him and me are bad enough, without him whispering to me in the store. It was nice though. I had to laugh. He asked me about you—this lined book he thinks is going to make me feel better—and he lectured me about not writing all my emotions down when I wrote in here. It'll clear my thoughts he said. Ha!

I thought he'd be happy I'd started my 'journal' as he put it, but instead he said if I avoid putting down what I'm really thinking, then I'm only fooling myself. How would he know what I write if it's a secret journal?

There is a danger to writing what I'm feeling, my fears, my worries. If I do write what I feel... really feel...and Sammy finds this. I am so dead. Things are bad enough already.

James won't have me in his house anymore. Not because the rumors are true, not even because his wife believes them...she doesn't. She even stood nearby in the store to ward off the nosy parkers who would dare try to listen to James speak to me. It's his kids. He doesn't want *his kids to hear the lies, think badly of him.*

*James says he's protecting me. I know who from. Maybe he's wise to do so. He was horrified when I reached for a can of sauce and he saw the bruises around my upper arm. He started shouting about Sammy, how he should be stopped. Made it worse. He had to be pulled away. Elise was mortified. That's when she told me, she didn't believe the lies. She knew James hadn't done any more than try to help me. That's when Elise told me to stay away from her husband. That's when I had to leave the store, ashamed of my tears.*

*I had to walk past Masie, who crowed with pleasure at my sorrow. Masie—the root of all my evils right now. Even Sammy's brand of evil cannot compare. Some days the sweet face of my innocent, blue eyed girl cannot take away the pain I feel. Physical hurt I could deal with. I've done it every day. The mental pain at losing my mentor, even Holly's smile cannot fix this.*

*Masie seems to follow James around like a bad smell, even though she knows I'm watching. She doesn't care. I'm sure she's the hand behind the whispers. What better ruse to hide your own discretion than to blame another? Ever since I caught them two, ugh, I hardly can bear to think about it. If Elise had been the one to find them, not me, there would have been hell to pay. She walked in on them, catching them half naked in the room behind the hall, James shocked and ashamed, Masie with a strange, proud smile.*

*You'd think Masie would be grateful that I've kept my mouth closed, but she's not. Should I have started a rumor instead? Just walked away from their interrupted assignation and forgot I'd seen?*

*I wonder why my respect for James is not dead. I wonder why it hurts so much to be cut off from him. I think it's because he's the only true support and trust I've had that's been real. Apart from the pure love that comes from Holly, I have no other standard to hold true to. My parents are gone. My brother is so far away in New Zealand. Who do I look up to now?*

\* \* \* \*

*17th October*
*I'm watching Holly and Jack play in the back yard. The sun is streaming through the dining room window while I write. I remember laughing like that. Mouths wide open, laughter that seems to come straight from your belly and sing through the air. That innocence. Like the world belongs to you. The sun comes up in the morning so you can play, and only gets dark when you're tired at night. I remember running like that, feet hardly touching the ground, chest heaving, but never getting tired. They have no idea what real life is yet. I'm in my mid-twenties and I feel like an old woman. I intend to protect my girl as long as I can. Look at her. I can't believe something so beautiful came from a union like ours.*

*There was love once, though. That tingle in my belly, hiccup from my heart when I saw him. Sammy. I thought the sun shone from his every pore. His smile, his eyes. Hung from his every word.*

*Love.*

*God, I was so young. So naive. That first night in our marriage bed, I thought I had the world, by morning I knew I'd found hell. He cried. Said he was sorry. Said it'd never happen again.*

*It didn't for a while.*

*Help? What help? It didn't take long to know there was no place to run. I told Sammy's father once. What a mistake that was. Colin apparently 'talked' to his son. He told him to keep his wife under control. I ended up in bed for days because I could hardly move. Lesson learned for me—keep my mouth shut. Lesson learned for Sammy—any bruises inflicted after that were never in places people could see. Sammy made sure of that.*

*I'm free for an hour or two. Free to what? Sit?*

*I can't do much else. Sammy just left, apologizing, but still angry. He's heard the rumors. I told him they're not true, but when has he ever listened to me?*

*I hurt. I don't know how I'm going to make Holly her lunch when I'm seeing two of everything. I hurt.*

\* \* \* \*

*20th October*

*I don't know what's so great about an emotion journal. Everything I write is a complaint, a moan, a gripe.*

*I know the way things are here. As soon as people find something else to gossip about they'll go on with things, someone else will be a new pincushion for their barbs.*

*Take what's good in my life and make it better. James told me once a very long time ago that when I had children, I'd know what really mattered. He was right.*

*Holly. She's who's being affected. I found her under her bed this morning, hiding with that silly bunny of hers. Thumb stuck in her mouth, using her bunny's ear to rub on her cheek, tears rolling down her dusty cheek. Which reminds me—clean under the beds. Sammy will not be pleased if there is dust under the bed.*

*Holly hasn't sucked her thumb since she was a wee tot in the cot. She's been doing it a lot lately. It's our fault. She heard us fighting, again. I dragged her out and sat her on my knee, and hugged her tight. I looked deep into my little girls eyes, tried to tell her it wasn't up to her to worry about the grown-ups. That sometimes mummies and daddies argue.*

*They might be my coloring, but the anger in those eyes was all Sammy. She scared me for a moment, just a split second. That coldness, that fury in her beautiful blue depths. Tears that had been falling seemed to instantly dry on her face. Disdain. That's what it was I saw. I had to struggle not to push her off my knee in shock. Run from her. She told me to hit him back. My five year old. She said when Jack was mean to her, if he pinched her, she'd pinch him back. Hit him back, Mummy, she said. He'll stop if you hit him back. I had to hug her tight so she couldn't see my tears.*

*If it were only that easy.*

\* \* \* \*

*27th October.*
*Things are getting strange. Sammy*

\* \* \* \*

*1st November*
*I was almost caught with this damned journal. Sammy came home unexpectedly and I had to rush to hide the puzzle box, diary, pen. If he'd turned on the oven, this damned thing would have been toast. I was so very close to just throwing it under the copper and destroying all evidence. If Sammy ever finds it...I shiver to think.*

*I thought that the titillation and lies would have died down by now, but it's only gotten worse. I know it's Masie. She was delighted to inform me she'd make sure I'd never get anywhere near James again, that the community thought I was a whore and a home-wrecker. I wonder what the community would think if I told them it was her I caught with James. Her I found with her shirt off and James' hand on her breast, his mouth on her neck.*

*She cornered me in the square this morning. I was sweeping out the town hall, just like I do every Friday, minding my own business, trying to ignore the gossip from the old witches cleaning out the church across the square. By the time she was done with her tongue lashing, and left, I was* a quivering mess. There was a book I read about some dogs. A man who's name started with a P. Every time he'd serve them dinner, he'd ring a bell. Soon all he'd have to do is ring that bell and the dogs would come running. I feel like those dogs some days. Raise your voice and my tail goes between my legs and I run and hide. Cower like a scared little mouse. Where is my pride?

Masie insinuated that I've poisoned James against her, that it's my fault he won't see her anymore. She was furious, red faced, and virtually inches away from my face. I was dumb enough to open my mouth and talk back. I said that perhaps James thought being faithful to Elise was more the reason for avoiding her. I thought she was going to punch me, but she spat in my face instead. Like those dogs, I took it. Wiped my face with the back of my hand, and cowered like a good little trained mutt. Don't upset the handler, Celeste.

Masie laughed in my face, and left me a quivering spineless mess on my own.

It took me twice as long to finish work, and it took me the rest of the morning to convince Sammy I had been at work, and not with James. He only believed me after he actually called James and asked him himself. I was so humiliated.

* * * *

3rd September

James came to the house. He risked and is risking everything for me, but I have an escape. He's got friends in New Zealand that are going to take Holly and me in, that will hide us. Just until I get on my feet. He's given me a name of a man who's read my stories, my silly little stories. He wants to publish them...in a book! James says I can pay him back by continuing to write, that this man says I have a natural talent. He said I have to think of Holly now. He's right of course.

*She shouldn't be in the middle of this. I just never thought there was a way out before.*

*There is a yacht in two weeks. James has spoken to the skipper via ham radio, and he's agreed to take me to Tahiti. We'll fly from there. I'm so scared, so unbelievably terrified. Not of the travel, the expense to pay back to James, the new life. I'm scared of what's going to happen if Sammy finds out in the next fourteen days. I can't think straight, my mind is in a whirl. One minute I'm terrified, the next so happy I could cry. I just have to make it two more weeks.*

# *Chapter Eighteen*

Jack stood on the porch of Holly's house. Crickets chirped a frenzied good evening to the deepening dusk of the evening, the generator's dull roar across the valley echoing in the still night. All the doors and windows stood open, but the house seemed empty, devoid of life.

No lights shone inside. The dark interior fought against the last reddened rays of light that struggled to inch its way through the shadows of the banyan trees that shadowed the house.

He scratched at his smooth, freshly shaved chin. *I was supposed to come here after work. I'm sure Holly said to come here.* He put his hands against the door frame and called into the dark hallway. "Holly?"

A voice from inside, tired, frazzled sounding. "In here."

Jack kicked off his shoes and went through the house, flicking on lights as he went. "Where are you?"

"Kitchen."

She sat at the kitchen table, in amongst what looked like the remains of a tornado. A kitchen cutlery drawer hanging open. Dirty cups and plates on the bench. A cabinet pulled out, a hole in the floor, wooden box on the table. He switched on the dining room light, making her squint against the sudden glare.

"What the hell happened here?" He asked. She looked terrible, eyes puffy, cheeks tear stained. She held onto a blue, hard backed book, clutched at it, finger tips white she held it so tight against her chest.

"Cheryl and Kristy were here." She flipped the book down into her lap, stared, lip quivering.

He laughed with confusion, raised an eyebrow and asked waggling an imaginary cigar. "What did they do, trash the place?"

She forced a smile. "Ha, ha, funny Jack."

She smoothed the cover of the book lovingly in her hands. "We found Mum's diary. In the safe under the cabinet."

Jack picked up the wooden box on the table, slid the pieces back together, turning it over and around in his hands. "This is one of Dad's puzzle boxes." He pointed out a stamp, J.Q. under a thick layer of dirt. "Christ, look at the dust on it."

"Your dad actually told me to look for it. I just didn't realize it was under my nose the whole time. It's been right here since the day Mum died. The last date in the diary was the 1st of November. She...they died on the 15th."

Jack watched as she struggled with her emotions, running her hands through her hair, brushing it away from her face, mouth pressed firmly together. Her body stiff to keep from trembling. He wanted to take her in his arms and stroke her back. To let her know he'd never let anything hurt her again, but something held him back. She was struggling to find the words. He clutched at the table instead to hold himself back, to give her time to speak.

"God, she struggled with my father, with herself. She was so lost. Masie...Masie and James—they... Oh Jack, James was trying to help Mum escape." She stared up at him, eyes searching for a sign of understanding.

Jack crouched down in front of her chair, looked up into her face. "Can I read this?" He placed his hand on the book, a diary that not only had opened her eyes to her mother's secrets, but obviously held some of his fathers.

"Yeah, you need to. Your father loved my mother, I think, but not in the dirty way everyone thought. He was a good man, Jack. He made mistakes, but...He was the one person my mother could wholly trust." Holly put her hand on Jack's face, stroked his cheek, smiled at him, eyes full of sadness. "Like the way I trust you, Jack."

He gulped down a lump in his throat. Now he needed some time. What mistakes could have been bad enough to cause the pity he saw now in Holly's eyes. He forced a smile. "Why don't I read this after dinner? Sounds like we both had a very long day. Marty tried to keep me busy, take my mind off things, and ended up destroying half the work I finished in his rush to help."

"Oh, no. Dinner." Holly put a guilty hand to her mouth with a gasp, eyes widening. "I'm sorry, I read all afternoon."

Jack laughed. She looked horrified that she'd forgotten. "We'll whip up some sandwiches or something. Is the copper hot?"

"No, I've done nothing. After Kristy and Cheryl left, I lost track of the time." She leapt out of her chair and hurried into the kitchen, burying her head inside the large chest freezer, moving items around, mist of cool air surrounding her in a haze. "It won't take long to whip something up." Her voice sounded muffled as she dug deep down into the depths of the freezer. Her toes were barely touching the floor she was hung that far over. He couldn't help but laugh, clutching at his belly. The feeling of letting go felt so good after the last few hurtful days.

"You look so funny. You almost need a winter coat."

She popped back up and turned to him with a quizzical grin. "Do you want to eat or not, cheeky bugger." She turned back around and dug out a box. "We can have a cowboy dinner—beans, bacon and eggs. Just have to defrost the bacon, and we're good."

"Okay, I'll go light the copper. You pour us a drink. When the water's hot, I'll run you a bath. I'll keep you company while you soak. By then the bacon will have defrosted enough so that we don't have to eat it in blocks."

Holly smiled, crossed the floor and grabbed his face with her two frozen hands. He gasped at the shock and then melted into her embrace as she kissed him. As the kiss deepened he thought he may have to take her right there and then on the kitchen floor, but she broke the kiss and gazed with pure delight, into his eyes. "You are a good man, Jack."

He giggled to himself. *If only she knew what I was really thinking.*

\* \* \* \*

She sat relaxed back, sunk up to her neck in the bath, knees poking out of bubbles that layered the water's surface. The bathroom was hot, a cloud of steam sitting at the ceiling, hovering damp above them. A glass of chardonnay sat on the rim, and she sighed with pleasure.

Jack looked up from his position on the floor, diary open on his lap. She gazed at him, her head resting on a balled up hand towel, a lazy smile on her face. "This is heaven." Her face was pink, a sheen of sweat on her brow, but she looked happy.

He tapped the book, and took a sip of his own wine, placing it back down beside him. "This is hell. What your mother went through to cover for my dad and Masie. I'm so disappointed in him." He grimaced with pain. *I would never of thought it of you, Dad. I defended you to the very last.* He couldn't understand it. *Masie?* He shook his head. *I wish Mum had of been the one to find you, not Celeste.*

Holly swung around in the tub, hand grasping the edge, anger furrowing her brow, eyes glinting. "Don't ever talk that way about your father in front of me, Jack. Yes, what he did with Masie was wrong, but, what he tried to do for my mother... He was a good man, Jack. I won't hear another word against him."

Jack closed the book with a snap and placed it carefully on the floor beside him, tipping his head back to lie against the wall. He closed his eyes against his bewilderment. "I just can't understand it, Holly. He let your mother take the fall. He wasn't man enough to stand up to the lies. It was guilt that drove him, not any moral reasoning."

"I just don't see that. I see a man who made a mistake. I see a man who treated my mother with love and respect. I suspect there was guilt there, but he was a man who didn't want to see Mum hurt anymore. He tried to help her escape, Jack. He might not have been able to stop the talk—but he was there still trying to help her. He was proud of her, and I think he was scared for her."

Jack sighed and shook his head. "Masie has a lot to answer for. She played a big part in this, and the old bag is still neck deep in it. She's not changed a bit."

"You have no idea." Holly rolled her eyes. "Masie was neck deep in it twenty years ago. Cheryl told me Masie destroyed my mother's things after I'd left the island. My father's stuff was hallowed ground. Mum's—only good for the fire. Cheryl said it was like watching someone possessed." She shook her head, mouth set in a firm line, eyes glinting with determination. "I'm going to have to go and see her. She has to know that she's not going to hurt us anymore, Jack. No one gets to play games with my family, from this day forward. It's done."

Jack watched Holly slip back down into the water, relaxing again into the tub. Grabbing her glass of wine and taking a sip, bubbles slid down her slick, wet arm, and Jack's mind tipped sideways. His thoughts turned to a possession of another kind. *Holly included me as family. She has not once, yet told me she loves me. I won't force that from her. I know, in my gut she feels the same way I do. I'm a patient man. I'll wait for those three little words, but for her to include me as family...That is a big step for her. She's lost so much family already.* He felt his eyes prickle with emotion, and he knuckled at the corner of his eyes before she noticed.

He scrambled up off the floor, shucking off his shirt, unzipping his jeans and pushing them down over his lean hips. Holly, wine glass at her lips, eyes wide, choked out a laugh. "What are you doing?"

"Jumping in too. Suddenly, I feel *very* dirty."

Holly screeched with laughter, lifting her wine glass high, scooting back in the tub to make room. Water slopped and splashed out of the tub onto the floor with all the commotion. Jack, smiling from ear to ear, took her glass out of her hand and placed it on the floor, kneeling between her legs in the hot soapy water. Placing his hands either side of her head on the edge of the bath, he lowered his face to hers, kissed her softly on her lips, and whispered, "Yup, very dirty indeed."

# *Chapter Nineteen*

Holly stood nervous and shaky beside Jack, outside a perfect little cupcake cutout of a house. The sun shone, streaking hot against the back of her neck, birds sang cheerful songs from the tree's that surrounded the house. On this beautiful day, they should be out walking, fishing, in the garden, anywhere but here about to pull out more dirty washing from her past. Especially of someone who'd so clearly enjoyed making the most of her mother's pain for her own pleasure.

Waiting for Masie to answer the door she wrung her hands and tapped her toes, the basket slung over her shoulder bumping against her back with every jerky movement. The house wasn't what she'd expected. The broom leaning up against the doorway was. Long handled and long bristled, it looked like the classic witches broom. The house in stark contrast looked like Auntie Em's out of the *Wizard of Oz*. Perfect little paths led from the doorway to the road and from the porch to the driveway. Lined with precisely placed rock edges and bordered with flowers, the front yard was feminine and perfumed the air with floral scent.

Masie, when she opened the door, looked more of a match to the broom, than the house. Her short, curly grey hair was standing up on end, her face haggard, dark circles under her eyes. They narrowed as Masie took in her visitors, her now familiar scowl gracing her face.

"What do yorley two want?" She snapped. She leaned heavily on the door, looking as though she was both using it for support, and to block their way from forcing their way inside.

"To talk," Jack said.

Holly nodded. "We need to talk, about James, and about my mother."

Masie screwed her mouth into a sardonic smile. "Well, Jack. You've got no more use for me now yous father's gone. " She glared at Holly. "As for you, I never had time for yorley at all. So you can both just take yous selves home. Your mother..."

Masie screwed her face into a scorn of disgust. "I don't have even a minute to talk about her. She's not worth a second on my tongue or the dirt on my boot. Go home."

Masie made to move out of the doorway and close the door, but Holly was not having any of that.

She stepped forward, and pressed her hand against the quickly closing door, speaking in a low, cajoling tone. "Masie, we realize you loved James just as much as we did. Maybe...maybe more than Jack and I really even took the time to realize, until yesterday. I found my mother's diary—her journal. She explained in it how you felt about James. We *need* to talk."

Holly hoped desperately the half lie she'd told wouldn't backfire. Her mother hadn't written about love at all, but from Holly's personal interactions with Masie and James, Masie's affections toward the old man had been obvious.

It worked, to Holly's relief, her heart racing as she realized she may get the chance to speak her mind after all.

The door stopped with a jerk, and opened back up just as fast, Masie slack jawed with disbelief. "Your mother wrote about me? I don't believe it. I burned all..." She cut herself off mid-rant, mouth snapping closed, eyes narrowing.

*Yes, you said too much, but nothing I didn't know,* Holly thought.

Opening the door further, Masie stepped back with a sniff. "Yorley two better come in. Don't expect me to wait on yorley hand and foot. That stopped once I...we, lost yous father, Jack." She turned her back on them both and stomped up a dimly lit and cluttered hallway.

Holly looked back at Jack with a satisfied smile. He stared at her with raised eyebrows and jaw dropped, pure amazement written across his features. He whistled under his breath as he stepped off the porch and into the hall. "Whew, remind me not to forget you're a wily, wee thing. Fancy, getting us through the front door. I thought we'd be out on our ear by now."

"We almost were." Holly followed him down the hall, closing the door gently behind her.

\* \* \* \*

Masie's lounge was large and airy, full of furniture. A curio filled with figures of dolphins, whales, fish, and animals of all description carved out of Miro were hung on the walls. Masie sat in a large over padded chair, arms crossed, face as dark as thunder. Sitting on the edge of a ratty sofa, they perched on the edge. Holly dropped her basket at her feet.

"So, what do yorley two want? What more is there to say? James es gone. Past is past."

Holly frowned. "It's not actually. The rumors you started about Jack and me are recent. They're also patently untrue."

"Well, I don't know where yorley got that from. I don't start rumors. I don't listen to them either. I keep my nose out of other people's business."

Jack snorted with laughter. "Yeah, okay."

Holly shot him a look, digging her mother's journal out of the bag. "We know about you and James. We also know my mother, who found you two, *and* kept her mouth closed, took the fall for you. We know how you treated her. I'd say that was pretty deep in someone else's business, wouldn't you?"

Masie's lips sucked in so far, they almost disappeared into her mouth. She reddened from the roots of her hair to the tip of her bristly chin. "What lies—I'd believe no less from her. Trouble when she living, trouble when she dead." She shook her head, clucking her tongue against the roof of her mouth. "I can't believe this, being harassed in my own home. After all I did for you when you first got here."

Holly just about fell off her chair in surprise. Jack hiccupped in shock beside her.

Masie stuttered, "I leave yorley food, clean up yous house. Get no thanks for et either." She sat back in her chair, satisfied smile on her lips, crossed her arms back across her bosom.

"That was you? If I'd have known, you would have gotten a thank you—a warm thank you at that. I had no idea." *Now though, I wonder what else was on your mind? Were you looking for something else to burn while you were cleaning?*

Masie leaned forward in her chair and glared at Jack. "Yorley, what you playing at boy? I came every day to look after yous father—every damn day. I gave up me own life to look after him, so you could work." She sat back, sniffed, looked away. "I can't believe the gall of some peoples. Come into *my* house and treat me like some sort of pariah."

Jack stiffened next to Holly, and glanced at her. Holly nodded and put her hand on his knee in support. She hoped he didn't notice her hand shaking, nerves taut as a string.

Jack cleared his throat. "Masie, I know what you did. If you didn't come over every day, I would have struggled. I appreciate you coming every day. But—"

Masie jerked her head around, glaring at him. "What? No one

was going to look after yous father like I did. Don't talk rubbish, boy."

Holly could feel the couch vibrate with his anger, and she tightened the restraining hand on his knee. "We know you did it to help, Masie. We also know you did it because you loved him. What we can't understand is why you had to go out of your way to ruin other people's lives as a side show. Why did you burn my mother's things?"

"Why?" Masie's color rose. "James was blind before he get sick and after. Me an' him, we were together long before Elise gut her claws in him. Den when he marry her and start having babies he forget all 'bout me. Finally, when he see the light, yous mother stop et. Turn him against me. She needed to be taught a lesson. *Den* she think that she going to run away with him? No way in hell I going to allow that. Ruin them boy's lives." She stared at Jack, crocodile tears shining in her eyes. "I was looking out for you boys, you see."

"Wait—what?" Jack recoiled from her watery stare. "Who was running away from us? Celeste?"

"James was…James was going to run away with…" She pointed a shaking finger in Holly's direction. "Ha gal, Celeste. I heard him calling some ship up ha radio station. Calling ha ship fer stop, pick them all up." She shook her head, genuine sadness etched into her face, tears rolling down her face, through the lines in her face. "I told Sammy he needed to stop em. I was looking out for you boys, Jack. I swear, *I swear*, I didn't know he would go so far."

Holly's blood ran cold. Masie told her father James was running away with her mother, taking her with them. He was already a violent man, demanding and harsh with her mother, already suspicious of James. This would have pushed him over the edge. "James wasn't going. James was never going."

Masie stared, mouth open, eyes wide. "Course he was. I heard him. Telling ha ship he gut passengers to pick up."

"My mother and me, that's all." Holly flipped through the diary to the last entries and handed it, hands shaking to her.

She pushed it away, turning her face to the wall. "I nor need to see ha lies."

Jack leapt to his feet, snatching the diary from Holly's hands, thrusting it into Masie's. Tapping the open book, he hissed into the old woman's face as she cowered in her chair, fright bright in her eyes. "Read. It. Masie. You need to know what you did."

Jack hovered over the old woman as she looked from him to

Holly, back and forth. The book in her hands, shaking and jittering in her grasp, she put it in her lap, closed the book firmly and laid her hands across it, caressed it.

"*Read it*! You need to see, Masie! You need to take some responsibility for what you've done!" Jack roared, pain cracking in his voice.

"No. I will not read a word of ha gal's filth." Masie sat straight back in her chair. She was pale, face set in stone, fingers fluttering against the hard cover of the diary.

Jack snatched the book from her, riffled through the pages, hands shaking. "Well, I'll read it to you then. You'll know, goddammit. You'll know Dad wasn't going anywhere. He was helping Celeste get away...away from the man you helped...helped... ki—kill her." He dropped the book onto the floor, put his hands to his face, and groaned with anguish tinged pain. Masie, stared blankly ahead, neither acknowledging his pain, nor showing any emotion of her own.

Holly got to her feet, crossed to him, and pressed her hand to his arm. He shook with anger, face even paler than Masie's. He seemed fragile, fraught with emotion.

"Stop it, Jack. Just stop." Holly soothed, voice soft. He shuddered under her touch, and backed off a step. She looked down on the woman who'd cause so much havoc, pain, and unintentionally—death. A pool of pity stirred in her belly. *I actually feel sorry for her*. She thought with surprise. *She didn't get to experience the feeling of someone loving her like I have.*

Holly turned to Jack, placing her hands on his shoulders, wanting him to know it was okay, speaking only to him. Only he mattered now—only them, together. "This isn't helping anyone. James is gone. My parents are gone. Whether Masie takes some blame in any of this, or denies it outright, it doesn't matter anymore."

Jack dropped his hands from his face and stared at her in open mouthed astonishment. "How can you say that? If she hadn't told Sammy, maybe your mother would still be alive."

"Who knows. She may never have gotten on that ship. She might not have been able to survive in New Zealand alone. She may have come back. There are all sorts of scenarios, all different. Who knows what would have happened."

Tears gathered in the corner of Holly's eyes, a lump in her throat so huge it was hard to swallow against her own pain. She looked into Jack's eyes, his haunted face, gestured toward Masie. "Look at her, Jack. Masie was so in love with your father, she caused pain to salve her own hurt. I know it's hard to see right now, but she lost someone she loved too."

Jack ran a hand through his hair, gazed at her with pained disbelief. "I can't understand how you can forgive so easily."

Holly shook her head. "I don't think it's about forgiveness. It's about letting bitterness destroy you. It's what it's done to Masie. After all her efforts what has she got? Nothing. We have each other. She's alone. All she's left with are lies and deceit. It's not going to keep her warm at night."

She tugged at his arm, picked up the book from the floor. "Let's go Jack."

Masie stirred in her chair. "I loved him, you know, all my life. He married Elise and broke my heart once. He loved your mother and broke my heart twice. Then you..." She stared blankly at Holly. "You came back and it started again. I waited for him for so long." She stared blankly up at them, lip quivering, desperation glistening in her eyes, wet tears rolling down her cheeks.

Masie grabbed out at Jack's wrist as he turned from her, disgust and pity twisting his mouth into a grimace. He turned back and looked deep into her eyes. "You reap what you sow, Masie. If you wanted love you should have shown compassion instead of hate." Jack tore his hand free of her grip with a jerk and nodded to Holly. "I think we're done here."

# Chapter Twenty

*10th September*

*My dearest daughter,*

*If you're reading this, it means I'm gone. No longer able to hold you in my arms, kiss your sweet face. I won't get to see you grow into a stronger woman than I. It means I made the wrong decision, because—God help me—I'm terrified that it is. I've struggled to make the right choice—it's not only for me, but for the family. I have to do what is right, what I vowed all those years ago, for better or worse.*

*I have had a chance, an opportunity to make a new life, a life away from here, far away from what I know, from what I have been brought up to believe. One I've decided not to take, because my life is here, with your father, on this island I grew up on. The fear of the unknown, the insecurity of what could be, I'm just not cut out for that. I don't think I have the strength to start over. Your father and I...Things are difficult, but I love him, and he loves me. He loves us.*

*I hope it's the right decision, to stay, to fight back for our love. I can make your father see it, if I stay. If I go, I'm giving up. Giving up on what we used to have, what we could be again.*

*If not, there's something you should know that I want you to hold on to.*

*The best thing your father and I ever did in this lifetime was to bring you into this world. The one thing we did right. You have no idea the joy you brought us, and the happiness that came into our lives the day you were born.*

*What I want for you, my darling is a love better than what your father and I have. Ours is flawed, based on jealousy and interference, pain and heartache. I don't want that for you. You deserve better.*

*Find someone to love who will be strong for you, love you for who you are, no matter what. Grab it and don't let it go. If someone who is supposed to love you tells you you can't do something because they don't understand it, not to explore life because they don't want to be alone...run as fast as you can, because that's not love. Love is not easy, but it shouldn't be based in bruises and fear.* I'm not going to take that anymore. I'm going to be strong for you, make *sure you grow up in a loving family. If I do nothing else, this I vow to you.*

*If you find someone who will treat you like an equal, love you no matter what, love you with all of his heart, who would die before hurting you, you hold on to that honey. You never let it go.*

*I want to teach you so much, and show you the world. If this letter is all I have left, then I want you to live your life knowing how much you were loved. Oh Holly, so much. How much I want you to be loved.*

*I will always be with you. I will always love you.*

*Love, Mum XXX*

# Chapter Twenty-One

Holly crumpled the letter in her hand, eyes dry, and irrational anger burning a hole in her heart. She sat stiffly, toes tapping with nervous energy. *How am I supposed to take this letter? Touched because you loved me? Hurt because you didn't love me enough to leave?* She gritted her teeth against the pain, confusion that started to build. *Just when I think I understand you Mum, you throw a curve ball*, she thought.

Jack reached over from his seat beside her and gently pried the paper out of her hand, smoothing it out on his legs. "You okay, Holly?"

"Uh-uh, no. Read it."

Giving her a quick sidelong glance of concern, he bowed his head over the paper.

They'd returned from Masie's earlier that morning and had been unable to settle, Jack pacing up and down in Holly's lounge, wearing a track into her rug. She'd thought that the letter, still unopened would be a distraction, but now she felt like wearing a new path in that rug herself.

"Why didn't she go, Jack? Why the hell didn't she go? She had an escape and she made the choice to stay."

"Maybe she thought she didn't have a choice. She was an abused woman with nowhere to run. This opportunity to go might have been scarier than what she already knew. I don't know." Jack shook his head. "She obviously thought she could fix what she had here."

"What—a husband who beat her, and a child who used to hide under the bed?" The anger within her crumpled into dust. A deep shame spread through her. "She stayed because of me, didn't she? Ultimately I kept her here. I killed her." She dropped her head into her hands, leaning over her knees as a dull pain born from guilt, sliced through her belly.

Jack slid off the chair, knelt before her, lifting her face in his hands so he could look into her green eyes, dark with despair. "Don't do this, Holly. You were a kid. You didn't make this decision for her."

"She stayed for family, Jack." She searched his face for some understanding. His dark eyes held pity, mouth twisted in sadness.

"Celeste knew exactly what she was doing, what staying with Sammy meant. She would have known what missing this opportunity would have done to Dad. He would have kicked her arse from this side of the island to the other himself, when he'd found out."

Holly barked a mirthless laugh. "He never got the chance."

"No. The worst happened. Sammy found out and took both their lives." Jack cupped her chin, and put his face close to hers. "It was the wrong kind of love, Holly. Your father needed to control, needed fear to make sure Celeste stayed. That doesn't breed love, it seeds hate. If Celeste had lived, if they both had lived, they wouldn't have been happy."

"She made the wrong choice."

"She chose what she thought was love over the fear of the unknown. It's not wrong to choose love—it's never wrong. She chose the wrong man to love is all."

Jack pulled her to her feet, slipping his arms around her waist, looking deep into her eyes. Holly shivered under his scrutiny. "Your mother wrote that letter to tell you she loved you. That she wanted the best for you. Not to be bitter about her choices, that even she was uncertain of. She wanted you to make better choices. So make them. Make her proud by not making the same mistakes she did."

Holly stared into his clear brown eyes, and all the hurt fell away. *He's the one. I've known he was the one for a long time, and yet I've not told him. Mum said that when I found someone like Jack I should hold on. Hold on tight. She's right. Even if she did make the wrong decision, I shouldn't.* Her heart felt lighter at the thought, mind clearing of the thick fog of denial.

Jack stroked her hair, tucking a strand behind her ear and she caught his hand, bringing it to her mouth, and kissed it. She'd seen the pain of lost love in Masie, what bitterness could do to a closed off heart. She'd felt the true love of her foster family, the support of a loving mother and father in Bill and Tina. She'd known the love of a real family. She knew love. The torment of knowing her parents couldn't make their relationship work shouldn't shadow her own attempts to forge a future. *I will not make the same mistake.*

Holly looked into Jack's eyes and said the words. The words cleansed her heart of pain. She'd remembered love. She'd remembered pain. Now, she would be looking only forward, making a new beginning. One she hoped would bring a new light to her life,

free of shackles from the past.
      "I love you, Jack."

# *Epilogue*

They stood hand in hand, deep in the heart of the banyans. It was a perfect place to be. The photographer's knee's popped loudly in the silence as he knelt in the leaves.

"Okay, I need you two to stop staring at each other for a sec, and look this way."

Holly and Jack grinned at each other and turned to face him, their arms sliding around each other's waists.

"Kristy, adjust Holly's dress please. The train is all bunched up at the back." The photographer pursed his lips, camera held jauntily in the air. He waved it in a hurry up motion and pursed his lips.

Kristy hiked up her satin dress, tiptoed in her high heels through the leaves and sticks to Holly's side. "Ugh, you two had to come down here for photos." She bent down with a groan and fussed with Holly's dress. "There, that should satisfy Max. Jesus, Rosy needed to choose someone less anal about taking photos."

Holly dissolved into giggles as she looked down at Kristy still fussing with her wedding dress. "Shh...I'm grateful they're both here, and she loves him. Plus he's a professional photographer on Pitcairn. He can have all the tantrums he wants." She turned her eyes back to her sister standing proudly beside Max. Her eyes gleamed with happy tears, a smile wobbly on her lips. Holly blew her a kiss, then turned and gave her new husband a kiss too.

"Kristy! Get the hell out of the shot! Keep doing that. Argh, the light is perfect! Kristy! Move your arse!" Holly could barely hear his frantic voice.

Staring up into Jack's eyes, she could see love shining from his. Among the banyan trees, on this perfect day, in this perfect place, they found love, cemented love, and remembered love.

## About the Author:

Nadine Christian lives on Pitcairn Island, a small isle in the middle of the South Pacific, with her husband, five children, four goats, two cats and thirty chickens. With its rich maritime history, Pitcairn's romantic past comes alive in her novels, capturing the taste of life on an isolated tropical island, miles from the rush and bustle of normal city life.

Visit http://www.nadinechristian.com to learn more about the author and Pitcairn Island.

# *Also from Eternal Press:*

## Heartspur
by Nancy Lindley-Gauthier

eBook ISBN: 9781615727100
Print ISBN: 9781615727117

Contemporary Romance
Short Novel of 56,335 words

Jillian Trent falls for a cowboy—but not just a cowboy. He's a champion of reining...from Texas, from money, and realistically, far out of reach.

Or is he? The moment he asks her out, Jill starts to puzzle over his 'real' motivation.

After all, a trail ride through the Catskills, overshadowed by the legends of 'the Headless Horseman' might seem romantic to some...or it might highlight some of the dangers inherent to riding—and love. And she knows there is a danger.

Nothing is what Jill expected, though. She's fallen for a man and at the same time, become enchanted with a golden Haflinger. All her ambitions, for love and for her riding career, are at her fingertips. Yet, both are threatened.

Unfortunately, no one else shares Jill's perception. Perhaps, Jill's involvement in mystery writing makes her susceptible to seeing clues where there are none.

Will she put aside her self-doubt and trust? Or will that leave all of them in deadly danger.

# Also from Eternal Press:

## Stranger by Morning
by Adrienne Davenport

eBook ISBN: 9781615727063
Print ISBN: 9781615727070

Contemporary Romance
Novel of 73,562 words

An alluring combination of danger and temptation...

Since she was a young girl, impoverished Chicago resident Reese Donavon has known High born teen, Christian St. Lorraine. A friend of her cousin's, Christian has always harbored a tendency for getting himself into trouble. Still, Reese can't resist idolizing the handsome teenager. As she grows, so does her attraction for Christian.

Now a teenager herself, Reese's attraction for Christian has blossomed into far more than petty infatuation. For a time the relationship shared between the pair is nothing short of fairytale material. Until one day, having just graduated from high school, Chris goes off to college leaving Reese alone and confused.

Years go by without any sign of him. Now a reporter for the Chicago Times, Reese has spent much of her career tracking a world renowned thief known only by the sinister title "The Dark Angel".

Unaware of the criminal's true identity, she soon finds herself on her way to India, once more tracking the felon's activity.

# *Eternal Press*

**Official Website:**
www.eternalpress.biz

**Blog:**
http://www.eternalpress.biz/blog/

**Reader Chat Group:**
http://groups.yahoo.com/group/EternalPressReaders

**MySpace:**
http://www.myspace.com/eternalpress

**Twitter:**
http://twitter.com/EternalPress

**Facebook:**
http://www.facebook.com/profile.php?id=1364272754

**Google +:**
https://plus.google.com/u/0/115524941844122973800

**Good Reads:**
http://www.goodreads.com/profile/EternalPress

**Shelfari**:
http://www.shelfari.com/eternalpress

**Library Thing:**
http://www.librarything.com/catalog/EternalPress

We invite you to drop in, visit with our authors and stay in touch for the latest news, releases and more!

CPSIA information can be obtained at www.ICGtesting.com
Printed in the USA
BVOW022205270613

9 781615 728558